Dawn of the Night

Idazle Hunter

ISBN: 1463548265
ISBN-13: 978-1463548261

DEDICATION

To everyone who stood by me throughout Nanowrimo.

ACKNOWLEDGMENTS

Here's a big thanks to my friends and family who have encouraged me throughout this process. Thanks to the Writing Force and all of our members for critiquing and helping me get one step closer to my dreams! Y'all rock! And also, thanks to my awesome teachers, whether they taught me the history that I've twined into my writing or just the basics of how to write. I couldn't do it without you guys!

Google will forever be my hero for information! I never could have set up some of the ceremonies without it! Go Google!!!

Of course, this story would never have been written without Nanowrimo.com! This site really pushed me to my limits, but it was worth it in the end.

CHAPTER 1

The loud scream reverberated up and down the halls of the castle, getting louder and louder as the walls bandied it to and fro. The source of the cry was a small boy, only seven years of age. It was the dawn after his birthday, and as son of the great knight Sir Laurence, it was his time to become a part of the knighthood. Lord Ivan was already at the castle to claim his new page.

"But, Father!" the boy pleaded once more, tears streaming down his face as he clung to the man's waist.

"Now, now, Paul," Sir Laurence whispered, ruffling the boy's black hair. "Be calm. There is nothing to fear. This is a great honor! My own son is going to become a page!"

"I do not want to leave!" he screamed, pounding his fists on Sir Laurence's legs.

"That is enough, son," he replied with a stern look. He was only glad Lord Ivan had agreed to wait outside for the young boy. Certainly, this would have been embarrassing.

"Mother!" he cried, turning to the woman who sat next to Sir Laurence. "Please! Tell Father I do not have to leave! I can be the page to a Lord here!"

She shook her head. "There is nothing we can do about it, Paul," she whispered, kissing him lightly on the top of the head. "You are a strong boy. You will be fine. One day, when you are older, you can come back and visit us. We shall still be here."

He pouted. "He cannot take me!"

Sir Laurence knelt down next to the boy. "Your Mother and I have already agreed to let you go. It is set. You shall complete seven years of training with Lord Ivan. That is that." He looked up at his wife. "Please, Maria..."

Maria knelt down, though it took more effort than usual on account of her greatly extended stomach. "Lord Ivan is a great man. He will take great care of you over in Asthla."

"But Asthla is not Cahal!" he protested.

"You shall be fine, son. Stop with this dramatic nonsense," she said, giving a final kiss before getting up.

He began to inhale as though he was going to scream again, but Sir Laurence covered his mouth and muffled the sound.

"Come, son," he said, taking him gently by the hand.

Paul frowned and looked over his shoulder at his mother. She gave him a reassuring smile and placed her hand on her stomach.

"We will wait here for you, Paul. Your father and I, as well as your brother or sister to be," she promised, giving him a wave.

He tried to smile, but found it impossible to do under the circumstances. Instead, he wore a frown as his father led him out of the castle.

"Please, Paul. At least be courteous to Lord Ivan," Sir Laurence told him as they walked together. "He is a very nice man. I grew up with him back when I was a young boy. Of course, knighthood led us down our different paths, but we were never really out of touch. Just like you and I will never be out of touch."

"You will be out of touch! I will never be able to reach you!" he complained, tightening his grasp on his father's well calloused hand.

He chuckled softly under his breath. "You will not be able to touch me, true, but you can still send me letters, and I, you." He glanced around the hall. Discerning that it was empty, he reached into his pocket and produced from it a tiny whistle-like flute.

Paul raised an eyebrow at the sight, which got another laugh from his father.

"This is an old Hunter family secret," Sir Laurence told him, rolling it over and over in his hand. He stopped for a moment, showing a tiny carving on the base. It read, "Laurence Carson Hunter." "Should you ever find yourself in dire need to see me again, just blow this."

"It is a whistle! How can a whistle bring you from such a distance?" Paul asked.

"Do you remember nothing I taught you? Magic will show you the image of whatever it is that is inscribed on it," he said. "But do not show another Hunter! While the knowledge has been passed down for many generations, the use of it is forbidden for it supports the very thing others in our family seek to destroy!"

"Why are you not like the rest of our family, Father?" he finally asked.

"Because I know right from wrong, and I hope you do too. The creatures and magic of this earth are not terrible things. They are only terrible when used by the wrong person. Remember this lesson above all others, Paul. It will protect you from the Hunters who would bring harm to us. After all, the punishment for disobeying the Orion Clan is death, and I know you would not wish that on our family."

Paul shook his head rapidly. "Never, Father!"

"Good. Now, shall we continue our walk?" he asked, motioning to the hall. The gate was now in sight.

Reluctantly, Paul nodded his head.

"Very well. Come now, son," he said, walking slowly to match Paul's shorter strides. When they reached the gate, they were greeted by a rather chipper Lord, just nearing the end of his life's summer.

The man bowed low to Sir Laurence, and he returned the gesture, motioning for Paul to do the same.

"It is a pleasure to see you again, dear Sir Laurence," Lord Ivan said as he straightened and greeted the two. He firmly shook hands with Laurence before turning to the youth. "And you must be my page, Paul," he said, holding out his hand to him.

Hesitantly, Paul took his hand. "Good day, Lord Ivan," he whispered.

"Ah! Quite a grip you have there, Paul!" he said, beaming from ear to ear. "You will make a fine knight one day! Such a firm grasp of your sword hand!"

"Thank you, Sir," he said with a blooming blush.

"You are quite welcome, young man," he said, releasing his grip. "If you would not mind, Sir Laurence, I would like to be alone with Paul from hence point on. It is not good for a father to loom around for too long. We would not want him to get too upset at your departure."

"Of course, Lord Ivan," Sir Laurence said with a bow of his head. "Fare well, Paul. Remember: You cannot watch the sun rise if you have never watched it set." With that, Laurence turned on his heels and returned to the castle.

As soon as Sir Laurence left the courtyard, Lord Ivan's gaze became steely. "Now listen here, peasant boy, you will do what I say when I say it. You will not question my authority, nor will you speak unless spoken to. Is that understood?"

Paul nodded his head.

"Were you not just spoken to?" Lord Ivan hissed, flicking a scourge at his side.

"Yes, Sir. Understood, Sir!" he said quickly, watching the whip with eyes as large as trenchers.

6

"That is more like it," he laughed, holding it still. "Now, if you really want to be a knight, let us get this straight: Being a knight is not fun. It is not glorious. It is not very rewarding."

"But Father sa-"

He was cut off by a snap of the whip across his shoulder. As it bit into his flesh, he let out a scream of agony.

"Do not speak unless spoken to!"

"But you-" he was cut off once more by the whip. His lip quivered as he whimpered.

"Silence! It does not matter what your father has told you! Your father is a fool! Do not listen to a word he says. Now you may speak."

"Father said you were his friend," he said. It was his futile hope that that one thing would reign true and Lord Ivan would be kinder to him.

"Were, Paulie. WERE," he hissed. "Enough talk." He climbed atop his waiting nutmeg-colored horse. "You will follow."

"I do not have my horse," he inquired.

"You have two legs that still work. FOLLOW." He held up the scourge. Without wasting a moment, Paul shut his mouth and nodded.

The Lord did not say another word to him for the entire trip that day. Paul preferred this quiet state more than when the Lord spoke to him. Every time he did not reply, he was whipped, and every time he did reply, he was whipped. It was obvious to Paul that his father had no clue what he was putting him through. If he did, he would not have done it. Unless he did know... He did not want to think of it that way, but there was always the possibility.

By the time the duo stopped for the night, Paul's feet were throbbing with pain. He all but collapsed on the tree.

"No time to rest yet, boy! You must pitch my tent!" Lord Ivan instructed.

Paul grimaced. "I am tired, Lord Ivan," he whimpered.

"And I do not care!" he hissed, waving the whip threateningly.

He quickly got to his feet and fetched the tent from the horse. As he began to set it up, he could feel the whip slicing into his back.

"No, no, no! You are doing it all wrong!" Lord Ivan shouted. "Do it right!"

He made even greater haste which proved to be a huge mistake, for his continued attempts were mere follies. More follies meant more whippings. By the time the tent was up, his back was sore and bloodied.

Without a word, Lord Ivan went into the tent and shut Paul out of it.

Paul sighed and sat down by a tree. He looked at the nearby forest. The dark shadows seemed to be calling out to him to join in their evil deeds of the night. The moon's light made them appear as if they were dancing, enjoying great merriment while he sat down, cold, hurt, and weary. For some reason, the darkness that had once frightened him now seemed to be the most welcoming. After checking to see that Lord Ivan was soundly sleeping in the tent, he tiptoed over to the woods.

As he stepped into the woods, it felt as though the shadows were brushing against him in a comforting manner. He smiled as he felt a breeze blow away the tears from his cheeks. His eyes, light amber in the daylight, were now a muddy brown, and his tanned skin was near ghostly white. Before he even realized it, he had fallen asleep in the soft grass of summer. The usual sounds of the night that would send him into a sudden state of panic could not even wake him at that moment of peace and solitude.

CHAPTER 2

Sleep turned out to be a rather frightful place for the young boy. Dreams he had never had before haunted his every sleeping moment.

Before his closed eyes danced many gleeful shadows, frolicking around as though their very existence brought joy to them. Blazing red eyes peered out of head-like blobs atop their somewhat shoulders. Paul opened his eyes to watch the group more carefully, all the while wondering why it was that he could not join in the merriment. He quietly called out to the apparitions.

"Pardon me, good spirits!" he shouted, though it came out barely above a whisper.

The spirits ignored him and continued in their dance around him.

Once more, he tried to summon their attention. "If you do not mind!"

Still, he did not receive the response he had hoped for. The shadows merely danced farther and closer, changing their minds with every whim. Once, they came close enough that Paul could reach out his gentle hand and brush it against their foot, or at least what he thought to be a foot. This received the attention of the spirits.

"Hurrah!" it cried out, picking the child up and spinning in a circle with the boy in his arms. "A new shadow has come to join us! A little shade in the vast light to give relief to the suffering! It has been a long time since we have had one as full of life as you, Paul."

"How do you know my name?" he asked, trying to free himself of the grip.

"The light will curse you no more, dear Paul. The light will curse no more! Ah, glorious is the day that one realizes how bright they can be when in the shadows!"

"That does not even make any sense!" he complained.

The shadow creature just danced in a circle. "A new boy, a glorious boy! A child has come to join us! Huzzah, hurrah, a mighty yahoo! A child has come to join us! Our new boy, our glorious boy! You have come to join us!" it sang aloud.

The others around him joined in, doubling the volume. "A new boy, a glorious boy! A child has come to join us! Huzzah, hurrah, a mighty yahoo! A child has come to join us! Our new boy, our glorious boy! You have come to join us!"

"I am not like you!" Paul protested, freeing himself of the strange creature's grip.

It frowned, or at least that is what it appeared to be doing. "He is not ready to join us! We shall return come dusk tomorrow! He will be joining us! A new boy, a glorious boy..." it continued to sing as it danced out of Paul's sight. He shook his head and fell back asleep, unsure if he was ever truly awake.

"Paul?!?" Lord Ivan called out when the sun was only a moment's time in the sky.

The young boy continued to sleep, his arm wrapped around a young sapling as though it were a doll a little girl might sleep with. He barely even stirred. Only his tiny brow twitched at the mention of his name.

"PAUL HUNTER!!!" the knight shouted out once more.

Paul was pulled from his dark slumber. He looked around, certain he had heard his name. As he got up, he noticed a tiny paper in his hand. He tucked it quickly into his pocket. "You called, sir?" he asked, running out of the woods to meet his master. His hair was a mess, littered here and there with a twig, a leaf, or some other debris of the forest floor.

"You will come the first time you are called! Do you understand?" Lord Ivan hissed.

"Yes, sir," he said, bowing his head low.

"Now, take down the tent. We must make haste. We are expected home today. And make yourself presentable for once, you will, no?" he told him, turning on his heels to go tend to his horse.

With a sigh, Paul went over to the tent and began to fold, all the while keeping an eye on the forest. What had gone on in there last night? All he could think about was the note he had seen when he woke. Was it possible that those shadows could have handed it off to him? Preposterous... That was nothing more than a silly dream, seeming rather childish the more he thought about it. He assumed it to be nothing more than nerves. After all, he had never been away from his family for so long in unfamiliar territory with a new, unforgiving man caring for him – if what the man was doing could even be considered caring.

Looking at the woods in the morning light, he could no longer see the shadows that had haunted it the night before, even those he had seen while he was still certain he was awake. Instead, it was bright with white light filtering through the leaves rather than black shadows. Everything about it seemed peaceful, not feral as it was when the moon stood in the sun's place.

All the while he looked upon the forest; he could feel a nagging itch in the back of his mind, screaming at him to open the letter. When he could bear it no longer, he pulled out the paper.

"Join us," it read in a hand-writing barely discernible. "Mulcunya bayangan, jatuhnya cahaya. Bawa kematian untuk hidup."

"Well that makes absolutely no sense..." he mumbled, shoving it back into his pocket. Utter disappointment showed greatly on his face. He finished packing up the tent and brought it over to Lord Ivan with great struggle.

"Ah. You have actually completed a task properly," Lord Ivan said as he nibbled on a piece of salted meat given to him by King Richon of Cahal's chef. "Wonderful, wonderful." He tucked the tent back into the saddle bag and got back onto his horse.

"Pardon me, sir, but I am hungry," Paul said, looking up at the man with wide eyes.

"You are?" he asked with a laugh. "When we return, then you shall eat. Not before. Maybe that will keep those little legs of yours moving." Without another word, he hit the horse's flank with the whip and they were once more on the move.

CHAPTER 3

Paul stumbled along next to Lord Ivan. The legs of the horse were far too long for the boy's short strides. He was forced to sprint for many miles. Once, he did not pay attention to the path in front of him, and he stumbled upon a rock jutting up from the unforgiving ground. Lord Ivan was swift to halt his horse and dismount to castigate the boy. By the time he was finished, Paul was sniveling and crying out. From hence point forward, he kept a circumspect eye on the path, never letting it wander once to the sides for he was afraid of what he might see.

The sun was high in the sky when Lord Ivan finally decided to break. Once more, Paul collapsed on the ground. So far, knighthood was nothing like he thought it would be. His father had spoken only of the wondrous things that came with the title, never about the cost to become one.

Again, Paul was forced to look on as Lord Ivan ate, and not a single scrap was spared for him. Instead, he sat as still as the tall willows with their weeping branches, trying not to do anything to upset his master in hopes that Lord Ivan would give him so much as a crumb to satiate his groaning stomach or a sip of water to quench his sore throat. Of course, this was all in vain, for Lord Ivan finished and told him to get up to continue on their journey.

As they went on the move again, Paul thought about the shadows. They seemed so happy, yet he could not share in their merriment. Even when they tried to bring him into the joyful celebration, he still could not feel their delight. Then his thoughts turned to what the spirit had told him, something about the darkness being bright. The more his body ached, the more he began to wonder if what the shadow told him was reigning true.

Finally, he thought of the song. The spirits were actually praising him, using kind words of appreciation. He could say nothing of the sort about Lord Ivan, even though Ivan was supposed to be the light, the great Lord. Why was it that the shadows were so kind to him when no one else was? He shook off the thought and returned to focusing on the path. It was all just a silly dream. It did not mean anything. He was beginning to sound like the loathed gypsy fortunetellers, and he did not want to be associated with them.

And so it was that the two traveled the rest of the way to the castle in silence. Lord Ivan slowed at the first sign of civilization and stopped. He motioned for Paul to do the same before reaching into the satchel and pulling out a small piece of meat. He handed it along with a skin of water to him. "Eat and drink before we continue," he instructed. "You are beginning to look like the living dead." He shuddered.

Paul wanted to question the second statement but decided it was better not to. He graciously accepted the food and drink and downed both quickly while Lord Ivan draped a cloak around his shoulders. While he ate, he did notice that his skin was fairly pale.

"Welcome to Asthla, Paul," Lord Ivan said with a broad smile, the same one he had worn when speaking to Sir Laurence. It was the kind that never once reached the eyes.

Many people in the village looked on at the two in awe. "A new page!" "Look how cute he is!" "We will certainly have a wonderful knight in a few years!" "I wonder if knights still refuse to marry peasants..." were only a few of the things Paul could hear coming from among the crowd of onlookers. So this was the part that his father had grown to love. This adoration was certainly better than the hatred he had sensed would come with being a knight once he met Lord Ivan.

At this realization, Paul began to smile. Maybe things would turn for the better! Then, he caught the glimpse of a small group of men, hiding in the dark shadows of the ally. Their faces were shrouded by black, but their eyes shone through, a vibrant red.

"The light is the dark. The dark is the light," one of the men whispered to the other. "Join us... No longer will you be cursed by the light..."

No sooner did they appear did they disappear. Paul blinked his eyes, trying to find the men. Where were they? He began to slow his pace to try and catch a glimpse of them.

"Oh, Paul, dear boy," Lord Ivan called over to him. "Do keep up!"

Paul looked over and ran to catch up to the horse. He was surprised when he did not feel the scourge on his back. Then he came to another realization. This was all a show. Lord Ivan did not care about him. He only cared about keeping face with the common folk. That figured....

"You can expect some time with the whip when we are in the castle," Lord Ivan whispered so only he could hear.

Paul's smile began to fade, but at a nudge from Lord Ivan, he painted on a new one. The two continued on to the castle in their tiny procession, as fake as the performing puppeteer's puppets.

CHAPTER 4

Paul stared at the flickering flames, watching them dance monotonously to and fro. At least Ivan Averk, or so he had heard his master called, had the kindness in his abyss of a heart to let him sit by the fire. Though it was summer, the nights had been growing rather cold, especially within the confines of the castle walls. While the boy was permitted to be by the fire, he was not given a bed. Instead, he was forced to lie upon a coarse deer skin rug that was set at the foot of the Lord's bed. He had been instructed to lay there, rest, and when morning broke, tend to his master's horse, armour, and weaponry.

Due to the long trip, Lord Ivan went off to the land of dreams well before the sun went down. This afforded some time to Paul to roam the castle without his master's ever-scornful eye watching his every move, just waiting for him to do something wrong so that he might accost him and beat him soundly. There was now an aura of calmness around him, like the shade from the hot summer's sun.

As he walked down the halls, various knights walked by him. They gave him kind smiles that really seemed genuine, and occasionally they would greet him as they passed by. *Why is it that these knights were so different from Ivan?* he questioned as he watched them at their work. It was a refreshing change of pace from what he was used to.

One knight stopped as he passed by. "Hail, boy. Would you stop a while and come hither?" he called out, motioning towards him.

Paul stopped and hesitantly looked at the man. "Perchance..." he said, slowly walking over.

The knight raised an eyebrow. "What is the matter, lad? Be you afraid of me?" he asked, holding his hands up in an innocent gesture.

"No, no," he replied, shaking his head quickly.

He laughed. "Well, you have nothing to fear, child. What is your name?"

"Paul... Hunter," he stammered.

"Oh?" the man asked, raising an eyebrow. His brown eyes sparkled. "A Hunter?"

"Why? What does it matter to you?"

"My name is Asher. Sir Asher Hunter," he said, grinning from ear to ear now. He pushed his shockingly white hair out of his face. "You would not happen to be Laurence's boy, would you?"

He nodded. "How do you know my father?"

"He is my brother!" he laughed. "What? He never spoke of your Uncle Asher? I am hurt..."

"Father never spoke much of his family," he admitted.

"I see... I would not expect him to." He shook his head. "You know... I was just on my way out. Care to come with?"

"But what if Lord Ivan wakes and finds me missing?" he asked, terrified by the mere thought.

"Lord Ivan sleeps like a log, especially after drinking as much whiskey as he did. He will not be waking up any time soon. Besides that, we shall be back in plenty of time for you to rest and prepare for your work tomorrow. Maybe you shall be the first page of Lord Ivan's to actually make it through to become a squire," he laughed. "But... you have Orion's blood running through your veins. You shall fare quite well."

Paul had never heard his father talk as such about the Orion Clan. He never praised the Clan or the name that came with it. However, Asher seemed to speak of the Clan as though it was the greatest thing on Earth. Maybe his father was not telling him the whole truth. After tarrying on the topic for a while, he nodded. "I shall join you."

Asher smiled broadly. "Oh, joy! You shan't be disappointed, Paul! Mistress Ehiztaria will be thrilled to finally have you among us!"

He smiled. That did not sound too bad. Asher held out his hand, and he took it as they headed out of the castle and into the deepest, darkest part of the forest just to the east of the village.

Once in the forest, Asher walked over to a large oak tree, knocking on it in a series of loud and quiet raps. Strange noises could be heard from within as the tree's trunk opened up. A boy peered around the corner of the opening. "What is the secret word?" he asked.

"Chasse," Asher responded. "I come with a new recruit."

The boy nodded and stepped aside so the two might enter. Once within, Paul turned to Asher. "What does 'chasse' mean?"

"It is the French word for 'hunt'," he responded, leading him down a series of winding stairs.

They continued on in silence, followed by the boy who had answered the door. The stairwells were eerily quiet. As Paul looked at the walls, the shadows taunted him once more, writhing and twisting. Sometimes, they seemed almost as though they were reaching out from the walls, trying to grab him by the hem of his clothes or the tips of his hair.

Once in the room where the other Hunters resided, the strange shadow spirits fled, hiding in the hallway that housed the stairs. To Paul, they seemed as though they were frightened of the group, though he could find no reason as to why.

In the center of the circle of Hunters there stood a beautiful woman, golden hair flowing down her back in long curls, just dusting her hips. Her icy blue eyes turned on Asher and Paul. "Ah, brother Asher. I see you have brought us a new child. Speak, boy. What is your name?"

"Paul," he said, his voice barely above a whisper.

"Ah, yes... Laurence's son... How is he? It has been a while since I have seen him," she said, a bit of a poisonous sound to her words.

"Erm... Fine," he replied.

"I am sure Asher here has told you my name. I am Mistress Ehiztaria, current leader of the Orion Clan," she went on. "If the two of you would be so kind as to have a seat, we shall begin."

Asher nodded and led Paul over to two empty chairs in the circle where they sat down. Once they did, the boy from the door moved to the center of the circle. "Mistress Ehiztaria will now begin the meeting!" he informed the group. The quiet chattering that had been going on in the room ceased.

Mistress Ehiztaria nodded to the boy, and he moved to sit down in the group. "Thank you, Norton," she said before turning to address the crowd. "First and foremost, I would like to welcome young Paul to our meeting! He bears our mark upon his right hand."

The crowd turned to look at Paul who turned to look at Asher. "What mark does she speak of?" he asked, looking at his hand.

Asher touched three birth marks lined up in a semi-neat row upon the boy's right hand. "This is Orion's mark." He pointed to the same marking on his own forearm.

Eyes returned to Mistress Ehiztaria as she began to speak once more. "We shall now begin with a recount of the history of the Orion Clan as it dates back to my many times great grandfather." There was absolute silence as she continued.

"Orion was born many years ago here in England. Ever since the time he was little, he would entertain himself with hunts. He started with tiny mourning doves, shooting them down only with a sling. As he grew, his love for the hunt did also. By the time he was fifteen, he was addicted to hunting. It was that year that he took up a wife, another woman by the name of Ehiztaria. They bore a son, whom they named Hunter.

"One day when Hunter was older, he went into the forest to hunt for a deer with his father, a mighty prize to bring home. Hunter ran off immediately, but Orion did not worry. He simply continued on with his search for the beautiful stag.

"While on the search, Orion heard something rustling in the leaves, struggling. When he went to investigate, he came across the mightiest beast of magic: the dragon. It was clinging to a strange object, hidden within his claws. When it uncurled them, it revealed Orion's own son. Rage flared up within him when he noticed that Hunter was not moving nor was he breathing. As his anger rose, he brandished his sword and ran at the beast.

"The dragon would not go down with ease. With a single breath, it blew a plume of flames so hot that it scorched Orion's left arm to the point at which he could no longer use it. Enraged by this deed, he lunged at the dragon and soon after won. As he looked down at his terribly disfigured arm, hatred boiled within him, though not for a terrible cause. The dragon had caused him such pain, both physically and emotionally, that just killing the one dragon did not suffice to repay this.

"With this in mind, he began a group under his name, the Orion Clan with the surname Hunter given to all to honor his son, and vowed that they would get the vengeance that they so rightfully deserved. Daily, they would go on hunts, in search of any creature that possessed magic. The dragon had proven to him that magic was a terrible evil that needed to be destroyed, and the group set out to eliminate this wrong from the world.

"And so it was that our Clan was formed, to right this terrible wrong. Now, all the world knows of the Orion Clan, and many come from near and far to join this exclusive group. Those here, consider yourselves honored, for not many may sit where you sit." She made it a point to look at Paul. "You must earn your way in here."

Paul fidgeted in his seat. Now he could understand why it was that his father never wanted to be associated with these people. They did not even have a viable cause to fight for. Still, he sat through the rest of the meeting. Once it ended, however, he made great effort to be among the first to leave.

"We shall see you next week, Paul!" Mistress Ehiztaria called after him with a wave. For some reason, he highly doubted that.

CHAPTER 5

The duo returned to the castle not long after the sun had sunk below the horizon in the western sky. Paul waved a farewell to his uncle before going to his master's quarters. Sure enough, his master was fast asleep in his bed, not appearing to have stirred since he first went to rest.

The fire was now only a smoldering pile of embers, having long since gone out. Removing his cloak, Paul sat down in front of it once more. The embers began to look as though they were alive and taking on lives of their own, gaining eyes and mouths. "Join us." He could have sworn that one of the embers had spoken those words to him. "Join the darkness."

He rubbed his eyes. "Nonsense..." he mumbled to himself. "I am just tired, that is all. My eyes are playing tricks on me. I am not seeing anything..." He laid his cloak down on the ground next to him and rested his head upon it as though it were a pillow. It did not take long to drift off to sleep.

The shadow creatures returned in his dreams once more, though now they were a bit more humanoid. The one who had appeared to be the leader last time was the most human of them all. His black wispy form was now solid with dark skin. Long black hair fell down just past his shoulders, but his eyes were still a terribly vibrant red that seemed to peer through to his very soul.

"Paul Hunter," he said, smiling. White teeth became visible through this action, and they were as pointy, and likely as sharp, as the tips of daggers. "I take it you received our note."

Their note? What could he possibly be talking about? Then it struck him. When he last woke, the note was in his hand. He reached into his pocket and pulled out the note with the strange language on it. That was where it had come from! But how?

"Just read it aloud..." the man whispered, walking in a slow circle around Paul, gently tracing his shoulders with a finger as he did so. "Just read... Join us..."

"But I cannot read it. I cannot understand it," he replied, looking once more at the writing.

"You do not need to understand, only read. All of your problems will be solved if only you will read it," it replied.

Paul shook his head. "No. I cannot! I do not know what it is!" He put the letter away.

The spirit-man creature growled angrily, a cross between a feline and canine sound. "Take that out! Read it!" His hand was now clenched tightly on his shoulder, growing tighter and tighter with every passing moment that he did not make a move to take out the letter. "Read it!"

"NO!" Paul screeched, trying to break free of its grasp. "I will not read it! I WILL NOT READ IT!"

This only made the creature angrier. The human look was beginning to slip away as it became more of a wispy, shapeless form. "You will read it!" it demanded, now trying to sink its hand into his shoulder.

"I said no!" Paul screamed again, shaking his head back and forth quickly. "NO! No! No. No..."

He could now feel the sensation of someone shaking him, but it was not the creature. It had disappeared. Still, the shaking continued.

"Get up, good-for-nothing boy!" he could now hear.

His eyes slowly blinked open to reveal Lord Ivan standing over him, glaring fiercely. It would have been better had the shadow creature still been there. "Did I wake you?" he asked, rubbing sleep from his eyes.

"Did you wake me? Did you wake me!?! You could have raised anyone in this blasted village! Even the dead!" he shouted. He punched him brutally in the face.

Tears flew to his eyes as he held his hand over the now aching spot. "I... I... I am sorry!" he blurted out before burying his face in his cloak.

"Darn right, you should be sorry!" he hissed, kicking him square in the back.

His breath left in a sharp gasp. "Forgive me!" he pleaded.

"Oh, I shall forgive you! Once you have made up for all the trouble you have caused with your idiotic babbling! You speak to yourself as though you did not even know who you were! Idiot child," he growled, stooping low and pulling Paul's head up so that his tearful eyes were forced to look square into his own soulless ones. "Go sleep in yonder stables. I do not even want to see you until morning. Leave! Now!"

Paul scrambled to his feet, grabbing the cloak in a swift movement before Lord Ivan could change his mind and decide to give him some form of physical punishment. With speed like Hermes, he ran to the stables and lay down in the hay stash that was to be given to the horses at a later date. He caressed his wounded cheek and shuddered. Surely it would bruise and leave a terrible mark upon his face for days to come.

Nearby, he could hear the soft whinnying of one of the horses. It sounded almost as though the horse was sympathizing with him. He smiled slightly to himself and got back to his feet. When he followed the sound, he came across a black stallion with deep, soul-searching eyes. Gently, he patted the creature's muzzle. "Hey, boy," he whispered to it.

The horse turned its head slightly as though it were trying to get a better look of the boy. It whinnied once more, as if in approval of him.

"What is your name?" he asked, searching the gate to the stall. He could feel the slight engraving of his name. "Umbra?"

The horse began to neigh at the sound of its name. "Such a pretty name for a horse," he said, returning to petting it. "I wish I had a horse like you. Then I would be like a real knight! I could ride around atop your back, polished armour shimmering in the sun's light while the peasants looked onward, admiring me for once instead of looking at me as a child! Alas... That is but a dream. Lord Ivan will never help me to truly become a knight..."

The horse moved its head from side to side.

"What? Do you actually believe it could happen?"

It proceeded to bob its head.

Paul groaned. "What am I doing? I am talking to a horse! Surely if anyone should see me out here, they would think I am crazy..."

"I do not think you are crazy," a voice rang out from behind him.

He jumped and turned around, spotting a young girl with straight brown hair. She smiled at him. "I love to come out here and speak with the horses. They are great friends. Greater than the others in the castle," she continued, walking over to Umbra. She gently stroked the horse.

"What's your name?" he asked the girl.

"Silly pageboy! Don't you know who I am? I am Princess Dawn Rayland," she said, flicking her hair behind her shoulder.

"Sorry, Princess! Please do not have me lashed!" Paul said, quickly bowing.

She giggled. "You are cute!"

A blush bloomed upon his cheeks. "Pardon?" he asked, running his hand through his hair.

"Why would I have my father whip you? You did not do anything wrong!" she laughed. After a pause, she added, "And, besides, you are kinda cute..." She gave him a quick kiss before running off giggling.

Paul held his hand over his cheek and smiled. That was the Princess? He watched her disappear out the stable doors. "Farewell," he whispered under his breath. If Dawn came out there every night, he would not mind staying in there all the time. Her blue eyes seemed to hold his softly with a kind of sisterly love. He could feel a strange warmth in his chest, something he had never felt before.

After standing there for a moment longer, he returned to the hay stack. "Good night, Umbra," he said, waving to the horse. He could hear a soft whinny as he lay down and drifted off to sleep.

CHAPTER 6

When the sun arose the next morning, Paul was swift to get up. He went over to Lord Ivan's mighty steed and gave it some of the hay he had only moments before been sleeping upon. After a quick hello to the stable hands, he ran out of the stable and back to the castle. Luckily, Lord Ivan was still asleep when he returned to their bed chamber. His armour stood in the corner, awaiting him.

Under the bed, he managed to find an old rag that looked as though it had been used to polish his armour before, so he took it and began to buff the armour until it shined so brightly that he could see his own reflection staring back at him. Strangely, he still resembled the living dead. It must have been the hunger and lack of sleep that made him feel and look as such. Lord Ivan was still fast asleep, so he left the room and headed for the kitchen.

The chef was bustling around the kitchen and paid little attention to the mere page walking around the room. Relieved, Paul went over to the table where there was some food that looked as though it had been made the previous day. The chef made no move to stop him from taking a chunk of bread from the loaf and nibbling on it, so he assumed it was alright to eat it. It was certainly better than starving due to the lack of food from Lord Ivan. Once his bread was finished, he returned to the bed chamber to wake his master.

"Master! It is morning! Please rise!" he said, gently shaking his shoulder. "Please awake!"

Lord Ivan swatted at his hand. "It is not morning yet!" he groaned.

"The sun has risen! It is time to get up!" he tried again.

"Leave me alone!" He pushed the boy away as he slept.

He frowned. If he continued, he would be beaten. If he did not, he would be beaten. He decided it better to just leave him. After a quick glance around the room, his eyes settled on the armour. The golden hilt of the sword seemed to be beckoning to him. He just could not resist...

Moments later, he was jumping around the room, his master's sword slicing through the air. That was the part of knighthood that he wanted to know. He smiled widely and began to mock attack the wall. The sudden noise made Lord Ivan jump out of bed.

"PAUL!" he shouted, glaring at him darkly. He strode over and pulled the sword from his hands. "What do you think you are doing?" Taking the sword, he hit him over the head with the blunt edge.

He covered his head with his arms. "I am sorry!" he whimpered. "I am really really really sorry!"

"Why on Earth would you even think about touching my sword? This is not a toy! You want to be considered a knight? Never! Not if you keep behaving like this!" he scolded. He hit him again.

"I am sorry! Terribly sorry!" he whined again.

"Oh, you will be!" he hissed. Just as he raised his sword, he stopped. "And that is the proper way to hold your sword!" he said, placing on another fake smile.

"What?" Paul asked, cocking his head to the side.

"Greetings, Lord Ivan. Paul," a man said from behind them. Paul turned around to see that it was none other than the King himself. By his side was the young Princess he had met out in the stable the night before. The two children blushed.

Lord Ivan bowed and motioned for Paul to do the same. "It is a pleasure to have the two of you here," he said before straightening. "What is it that brings you around?"

"We are here to meet the new page that we have permitted to you," he said, walking over to little Paul. "Rise, good boy," he said, looking at the boy in the eyes. "What is wrong with your eye?" He gently fingered the bruise that had formed over the night.

"Nothing," he replied quickly, covering it with his hand.

"Very well," he said, turning to Lord Ivan. "Might I have a moment with you outside?"

"Of course." He walked outside with the King, leaving Paul and Dawn alone.

"What happened to your eye?" she asked as she walked over to him.

"Nothing," he repeated. He backed away from her slightly and kept it covered.

"You can tell me. I promise I will not tell anyone anything. Just tell me," she crooned, pouting at him. "Please?" Her blue eyes grew wide. "I am worried for you!"

"I just got hit... That is all," he said.

"Aw! Who would hit you? You are too cute to hit!" She gave him a quick kiss on his wounded cheek. "Better?"

He nodded, blushing even deeper.

"Mother always used to do that for me! I do not know why, but I just liked it! It made me feel so much better. How about you? What is your mother like? Is she nice? I bet she is nice... and pretty!" she babbled on. "And what about your father? You have already met mine. Where do your parents live? Are they far away? Will they ever come by to visit?"

He stared at her blankly for a moment. "Um..." was all he could say before the King came back in with Lord Ivan.

"Come along, Dawn!" the King called out to his daughter.

She waved. "Good bye, Paul!" she chirped before skipping over to her father.

"Farewell, Princess," he murmured.

Once the King and his daughter left, Lord Ivan returned to glaring at his page. "You told him, did you not?"

"Told him what, sir?" he asked, instinctively backing up.

"No matter... Come. Let us begin your *training*," he scoffed, leading the boy out of the room. "We shall start with *real* swords play, though you will not be permitted to use real swords. Then you shall proceed to learn about the lance and the javelin, and, if time permits, we shall move on to the battle ax. You will not ask for breaks, and you will do as you are told. Do you understand?"

Paul nodded. "Yes, sir."

"Then let our training begin!"

CHAPTER 7

This was the trend for the next seven years. The boy was put through many terrible trials, all of which he managed to find some way to overcome. Every time he knew there would be a meeting of the Hunters, he was certain to hide from his uncle. Of course, his uncle never persisted because he knew that Laurence had already poisoned the boy's mind with thoughts of peace and kindness towards all creatures. As for the shadows in his mind, they had become frequent visitors, though he never read their note.

Over the years, his body had changed so much. He was much taller, with greatly increased muscle mass. His body looked less like a child and more and more like a man. This greatly pleased him. The Princess was also growing up to be a beautiful woman whom he greatly admired. As they both grew, so did their love for each other. Needless to say, they both knew that there was little hope for their love.

Paul was thrilled to learn that, on his fourteenth birthday, he was no longer under Lord Ivan Averk's custody, but his joy was short lived. He was told who his next master would be, and he wanted to scream but had learned it better not to. His master would be none other than his uncle, Asher.

"Please! Tell me it is not true!" he begged Princess Dawn.

"Why are you so afraid? Sir Asher is a wonderful knight! He has even agreed to work with you one on one rather than in a group as is customary," she replied. "This is wonderful, is it not? Surely he will not beat you!"

"But I cannot work for Sir Asher!" he moaned.

"Of course you can! Besides that, my father will not give you any choice. You will have to work for Sir Asher regardless."

Paul just shook his head. "Why..." he mumbled to himself over and over again as he went to his new quarters.

Asher was swift to greet him. "Ah, nephew! How grand of you to join me!" He motioned him to come into the bedroom. "Right this way! Here... Put that stuff right here... Perfect!" he said, leading him around the room. Unlike Lord Ivan's room, there was another bed in this room. "I had some friends of mine bring that in last night," he said, noting that the bed was where Paul's eyes had shifted to.

"Thank you," he said, keeping his responses to the bare minimum.

"Where have you been the past years? I have been trying to find you! Mistress Ehiztaria has been very worried about you! Nonetheless, we will resume attending the meetings weekly. We will also keep up with your training. Of course, I shall have to treat you like a squire when we are out and about, but in here, you are my nephew." He lay down on one of the beds and watched Paul. "Getting a bit pale there, are you not?"

Paul shrugged it off and lay down on the other bed. "It is nothing," he said, completely dismissing it.

"Very well," he sighed. "You should get some rest. We have a long day ahead of us!" He was already getting under his blankets. "Good night, Paul!"

"Good night, Uncle," he replied, staring up at the ceiling. As he watched his uncle, he could not help but think about his father and the last conversation he had had with him nearly seven years ago, the only time he had ever used the whistle.

It was well into autumn, and leaves were beginning to turn brilliant shades of red and orange. Lord Ivan was out on business that Paul did not need to be around for, so the little boy hid in the stables and pulled out the whistle from his father. He gave it a quick blow, and a small cloud of smoke poured out of it. The image of his father appeared on the other end, though something seemed wrong. His father's usual smile was replaced by a hard frown and tears of sadness were welling in his eyes.

"What is wrong, Father?" he asked, watching his father's frantic form.

"It is your mother! She went into labor, and fell asleep. She never woke up! She is not breathing, Paul! Maria is gone!" he sobbed.

Paul blinked back tears from his own eyes. "Not Mother... She is strong! She should have made it!"

Sir Laurence shook his head. "Afraid not, son. Your sister survived, however." He held up a tiny girl dressed in a little red dress so that Paul might look at his new sibling. "Her name is Ammira Laura, meaning Princess with strength."

Tears began streaking down his cheeks. "I do not care about her! I want Mother! Why would that little creature survive and not Mother?"

"Paul... She is your sister! You should love h-"

"I do not care about her! I want Mother!" he cried out again.

He tried to speak again but was cut off as his son snapped the whistle in his hands.

"Curse that baby!" Paul cried out, dropping the whistle to the ground. "I will never love Ammira Laura Hunter!"

This memory brought tears to his eyes. He was hoping that he would one day be able to return home to see a smiling Mother and Father waiting for him upon his return. Sadly, that day would never come now, thanks to that pesky little sister of his. He curled up tightly on the bed. He still hated that girl, and he knew he always would. As the years went on, that hatred burned more and more and now, having to live with his father's own brother, the hatred was only kindled more. He closed his eyes and actually willed the spirit-man to come to him in his sleep.

CHAPTER 8

Sure enough, the spirit-man came to him as soon as he fell asleep. "You called?" he asked, a smile playing across his lips.

"What is it you want me to do?" Paul asked him, courage coursing through his veins

"Ah... He comes to join us at once!" it cheered. "Take out the note! The note!"

He nodded and pulled it from his pocket. "Just read it?" he asked.

"Just read it," he replied. "All of your troubles will be over! You will no longer be cursed by the wretched things of this world!"

After taking a deep breath, he began. "Mulcunya bayangan, jatuhnya cahaya. Bawa kematian untuk hidup." As he read the last word, he could feel his body begin to tremble. His legs buckled out from under him. "What have I done?" he cried out to the shadow creature.

"Exactly as I have always planned you would!" it laughed, jumping on him. The two began to merge into one: arms, legs, torsos, and heads all fused together as one body.

Paul screamed throughout the entire transformation. "Please! Stop!" he shouted, clutching his head. It felt as though his whole body would explode within moments.

The creature only cackled, throwing back its... their... head as it howled out in joy. "Thank you, Paul! Thank you ever so much!"

Paul opened his eyes to leave sleep. "What have I done?" he whispered, staggering out of his bed. He peered into the looking glass on the wall of Asher's room. His skin, if pale before, now seemed to be whiter than the winter snow, and his eyes darker than charred coal. "What have I done?"

He could now hear the spirit-man's voice within his mind. "You have done that which I have instructed you to do! You have become one with the darkness and the spirit realm! Now, just sit back and let me take control."

Paul had no clue what that was supposed to mean, but then he felt his knees give way beneath him once more. His mind began going blank with searing pain. "Get out of my body!" he screamed as spots formed before his eyes.

The creature within him only laughed at his pain. "Stand aside!" he repeated, as though Paul really had any choice. "You summoned me to you, now I will take the reigns!"

"No... No... No..." he mumbled. He clutched his head firmly between his hands as he moaned in pain, though it only lasted a little while longer. After that, he felt nothing and could not think of anything, lest it was through the demonic spirit within him.

"Paul? Child? Nephew? You alright? Wake up!" Asher shouted, shaking the sleeping boy as he tried to bring him to his senses. "Why are you sleeping on the floor? Come now, that bed cannot be that uncomfortable! Up and at them!"

Slowly, the boy blinked his eyes open and looked up at his uncle. "Good morning, Asher," he said, his voice rather strange. The spirit continued to try to get used to the strange workings of this new body. Meanwhile, the real Paul, whom became little more than a conscience to the spirit, could now understand why it was that he was not supposed to deal with such creatures as the spirits.

"Are you okay, Paul? You look even paler than before! I can practically see your bones through your skin!" he said, grabbing the boy's hand and holding it up to look at it better.

"I am fine, Uncle. There is nothing to worry about," he replied, pulling his hand away from him and flexing his fingers to get good use of them. With a bit of struggling, he returned to his feet. He looked at him with black, soulless eyes. "I am hungry, however."

"Of course. Come, let us eat," he said, wrapping his arm around his shoulders and leading him out of the bed chamber. "That ought to put some color back into you."

They walked down to the kitchen where the knights were already gathered and eating breakfast and chattering boisterously with one another. "If you ask me, I believe that the broadsword is the wisest weapon of all to choose. It gives power and strength!" one knight argued.

"Nay, sir! It is the daggers! They have a far greater accuracy than any sword, and it is far more agile. What say you, Asher?" another knight responded, turning toward his white-haired companion.

"I agree with neither of you for a simple sword with a shield would suffice for any battle. Not only do you have accuracy and power, but you also have defense on your side," he said, pulling two chairs over to the table for himself and Paul. "What about you, Paul? What is a squire's opinion on such matters?"

"I would have to agree with the use of daggers. They allow for far simpler attacks and methods of defense," Paul stated.

"Ah! The lad has a good head on his shoulders! He shall make for a fine knight, indeed!" the second knight laughed, clapping the boy on the shoulder.

"Daggers are such an underhanded approach to everything, though! That is the weapon of choice for the assassins and thieves out on the street! They have no place among the honorary knights!" the first knight stated. "Now the *broadsword* on the other hand! That is a wonderful weapon for any knight! That shows some strength!"

"You are looking at it all wrong. You should not look at it as how the underhanded use it, but as the noble would use it. Just because something is wrong in the hands of one, does not mean it is wrong in the hands of all!" Paul pointed out.

Asher smiled. "You are a very wise child, indeed. Where have you learned such things?"

"I have my resources," he replied with a smirk. Being among the dead for so long and learning from previous knights certainly counted as a resource, did it not? He knew better than to say it straight out that he was a spirit in a child's body. There was no need to cause a commotion again.

"Well... We shall just see how those resources help him out on the field, no?" the first knight said. He smirked. "Do you even know how to wield these weapons of which you speak?"

"Most certainly. Learning to wield them is like learning to walk. It just comes naturally. Whether or not I could actually win a duel is another thing," he replied.

"The King has ordered us to battle tomorrow. It will prove to show how much you really know about what it is like to be out to war! Hopefully, Asher will be able to keep you alive!" The group of knights laughed at such a comment.

"I am sure that both of us will be perfectly fine!" he laughed. "If anything, I might have to keep old Asher alive."

Asher joined in on the laughter. "We shall see about that, boy. After all, you will not actually be doing any of the fighting! You are a squire. You will serve by my side, but that will be all."

"So you say now..." he mumbled, inaudible to anyone save himself.

CHAPTER 9

After breakfast, Asher took Paul out to the training grounds. "Let us see how well Lord I-am A-jerk... Ahem... I mean... Ivan Averk," Asher said, clearing his throat, "has taught you." He tossed him a sword, and not a wooden one that was used for the training of a page. He himself also picked up a sword. "En garde!" he said.

It was a bit strange hearing his uncle speak French, but, nonetheless, he held up his sword.

"Perfect. Now, come at me and try to land a hit," he said, motioning him to come forward.

He nodded and ran forward, though he did not go in a beeline toward his front. Instead, he flanked him and aimed for the side. There was a loud crash as the two steel blades met.

"Excellent, Paul!" he said.

Ignoring the praise, he swung again, this time for the legs. Asher was quick to jump over the blade, leaving him very vulnerable. He swung the sword up and stopped just as it touched his boot.

Asher smiled broadly. "So I see you have learned well, but how is your defense?" He began to take the offense and swung at Paul's chest for a simple starter.

Raising his sword ever so slightly, he hit Asher's sword and twisted, pulling the blade right out of his uncle's hand. He caught it and held the two pointed at his throat. It was amazing what this spirit could do now that he finally had a host body! Never before had he expected to have so much potential.

With a laugh, Asher clapped his hands. "You shall make a fine knight a few years from now. Asthla will be lucky to have you!" After a pause, he added, "And so will the Orions."

"And I will be happy to join in their ranks," Paul stated with a smile. "That goes for both."

"Excellent! Our meeting is tonight, so we do not have much time... We shall have to skip the rest of your knight training for today. You have to catch some kind of magical creature. I have heard unicorns have traversed the neighboring forest. Perhaps you can catch one of those to bring to Mistress Ehiztaria. That would certainly please her," he mumbled, grabbing a bow from the weapons supply as well as a quiver of arrows. "Hold onto those swords. They might come in handy."

"But why must I go on a hunt? I did not have to the last time," he pointed out.

"You've been gone for a while. Mistress Ehiztaria no longer trusts you. We need to bring back a prize for her..." He handed him some of the objects he had been gathering. Soon after, they left the training grounds and began heading towards the forest.

Once there, Asher handed everything to Paul. "It is up to you to do this on your own. I am only here to make sure that you make the kill yourself. Only after that is done may I help you."

"That should not be a problem, Asher. After all, it is just a unicorn. I could kill one of those in my sleep," Paul laughed.

"Do not get too sure of yourself now, Paul. It is not as easy as you think."

"Sure, sure. We shall see about that," he said, ducking off into the woods ahead of his uncle. He could already hear the footsteps of a hoofed creature not too far off. If he was lucky, it would be a unicorn.

Sure enough, Lady Luck was on his side. There were not one, but five glorious beasts in the small clearing. He focused his gaze on one whose fur was the colour of the night sky and whose horn looked as though it had been carved out of pure pearl. It was the perfect catch for any Hunter.

He glanced over his shoulder. Asher had not caught up with him yet. This posed to be the perfect time to try his new abilities. After all, no one was watching him. He could do as he pleased.

The sun cast many shadows onto the ground in the forest. If he could control them as a spirit, there was nothing saying that he could not control them in a human's body. He lifted his hand and focused on the target unicorn's shadow. When he willed it to rise, it rose. A smirk played across his lips. He quickly clenched his hand shut, and the shadow wrapped itself around the unicorn's throat, choking it to death. The other four unicorns started in alarm and began to flee with nervous brays to each other.

"Asher! Asher! I got one!" Paul shouted, stabbing the unicorn with an arrow to make it look as though he had actually shot it with the bow rather than just strangling it with its own shadow. "Asher! Come quickly! Asher!" he called out once more.

Asher came running into the clearing. "There is no way you got o-" he stopped short. "I do not think you could have gotten a better kill than that." He knelt down and pulled out the arrow covered in fresh blood. "Wow... Directly through the heart... Mistress Ehiztaria will certainly be pleased! That means she will be pleased with me! Oh, happy day!" he chirped. He gazed at the sun. It still stood high in the sky. "We will not be meeting for a while. Take the horn as a token of your victory. The rest we shall leave. We do not want anyone to see us with such a beast in town."

The boy nodded curtly and proceeded to slice the horn off the unicorn. It proved to be a more arduous task than he had expected, but he managed to get his reward. He held the crystalline horn in his hand and smiled broadly. That *was* his reward! This human body was proving to be more useful than he could have ever hoped, even if it was a mere child's body. He tucked the horn into his pocket and followed Asher back to the castle.

"Perhaps we shall start with a lesson and then move on to matters concerning the Orion Clan meeting tonight..." Asher mumbled as they walked.

Paul shook his head. "We should spend more time with the clan's work. I hardly know a thing about it," he said.

"Oh, yes. I forgot. Old brother dear did not believe in the ways of our family. How he managed to evade us for so long is beyond everyone in the clan. Most people who disobey us... well... let us say... are never heard from again. Your father, however, keeps coming back to bite us in the butt about how wrong our beliefs are. It is truly a terrible thing," he grumbled, shaking his head.

"You are saying Father should be dead by now?" Paul asked.

"Aye, Paul. It is just the way of the clan. I am terribly sorry."

"Do not be sorry. It is perfectly fine by me," he hissed. The spirit had been following up on Paul's life the entire time, never letting anyone notice. He knew all about that final talk and about how much it was killing Paul that his father no longer paid any mind to him. The child had never received a letter from him, nor did his father ever visit when in the area. That anger was what led to his possession.

"Oh? So then perhaps this might interest you... The battle that we are going to is indeed a false fight. It has been 'issued' by Sir Pedric of Cahal. He is friends with King Richon's brother. Supposedly, they are trying to remove some of the men from his knighthood so that the throne will be theirs for the taking. Do not let the other knights know of this, for they believe it is to be a true battle. Sir Pedric has even notified me that a certain Laurence Hunter will be present at this battle," Asher whispered.

There was a look of mischievous delight in Paul's eyes. This was the perfect time not only to prove his worthiness as a knight, but to teach his no good father a final lesson that he would never forget as he had forgotten about his one and only son whom was sent out into the care of a terrible Lord. "My lips are sealed, Uncle."

"Marvelous! Now, let us prepare for tonight's meeting, shall we?" Asher beamed down at the boy. "There are but a few other preparations that must be tended to before you can officially become a member of the Orion Clan rather than just a nominee like the other members of the family who are not fit to fight but still belong to the organization so as not to be sentenced to death. First of all, there are your clothes. Not very logical for a Hunter..." He tutted at Paul's peasant-like clothes.

Paul nodded. "It would be far better to be dressed much like yourself. There are no places in this outfit to store weapons."

"Exactly." Asher pulled a dagger from a hidden pocket in his pants to prove the point. "I am sure we have something that will look decent on you, though it might be trickier considering white would only make you look like a phantom." He laughed and shook his own white hair that was the same colour as his entire outfit. "I am sure there is some black somewhere that would look far better on you..."

They arrived at the castle and strolled in, heading straight for the bed chamber. Once inside, Asher moved to a chest in the corner. "These are all of my clothes from when I was your age. Mostly white but I know I had some black in here somewhere..." He sifted through the clothes a moment longer before pulling out a black tunic and a pair of matching pants. "Perfect! Here! Put these on!" He passed them over to Paul.

Quickly, Paul changed out of his old clothes and put on the ones Asher had just handed him. He began to feel around them, searching for hidden compartments. He found two pockets at the waist of the pants, a tiny loop on the hem of the tunic, and a few other miscellaneous pockets of varying sizes in varying places.

Asher smiled broadly. "Now that is how a Hunter should dress!" He clasped the boy on the shoulder. "Mistress Ehiztaria will be so proud of you! And your father would go fall in a ditch!" he laughed.

Paul laughed with him. "For all I care, he most certainly could."

CHAPTER 10

Night came before the duo knew it, and they were sneaking off to the tree with the hidden entryway. Once more, they were greeted by the boy, and once more, they were led down the long hallway to the meeting room. Mistress Ehiztaria covered her heart with her hand at the sight of the two men walking in.

"Why, Paul! I did not think we would ever see you again! Oh, joy! Come, come!" she beckoned for him.

Hesitantly, Paul walked over to her, and she pulled him into a hug, not typically custom for one in her position to do, but, nonetheless, she did it.

"What made you decide to come back?" she asked, playing the innocent card.

"I have decided that the Orion Clan is the proper way for a Hunter's child to go," Paul stated. *That, and I am pro anything that is against that blasted Laurence!* he added in thought.

"Splendid! Truly splendid!" she chirped, clapping her hands.

"Paul, show Mistress Ehiztaria your prize from today's hunt," Asher prompted, nudging the boy's shoulder.

Paul nodded and produced the pearl horn from one of the pockets of his pants. He held it out in offering to Mistress Ehiztaria.

She gasped in sheer amazement. "You caught a unicorn today?" Swiftly, she turned to Asher. "What part did you have in all of this?" she asked, raising an eyebrow. "Speak the whole truth!"

"I only supplied him with a sword and bow. He made the kill and claimed his prize," he replied curtly.

"So I see... We shall have to induct this boy into our ranks! That should not be a problem. We shall just have to wait for the next full moon which should not be too long from now, judging by the moon's current size," she said, pondering as she spoke. "And you will need to bring your prize with you... and some new clothes, and *not* your uncle's old hand-me-downs."

When Paul looked at Asher, he merely shrugged.

"And you will need to bring a weapon you own. I am sure Asher can help you acquire one. Other than that, we shall take care of the rest!" She smiled. "Alright. So, with that settled, take a seat and the meeting will begin!"

All throughout the meeting, Paul found it difficult to focus. Those silly Hunters! They did not even realize they were letting one join them who was the embodiment of the very thing they hated! Perhaps this group was not as skilled as they claimed to be. Never the less, he would gain much from being among the inner workings of the Orion Clan. While their detection skills may have been low, their fighting techniques were legendary in other lands where the Orion Clan was only a faint whisper. With these moves on his side, defeating any adversary would prove simple, whether it be his father, his sister, or anyone else who got in his way during his process of taking over.

At the end of the meeting, Mistress Ehiztaria approached Paul. "Where was it that you made your first kill?" she asked.

"The clearing just to the south of here," Paul said.

"Then that is where we shall meet in a fortnight. The moon should be at it largest, and you should have adequate time to gather the necessary supplies."

Paul nodded. "In a fortnight it is," he replied.

"Farewell, young Paul. May the heavens shine down on you and bring you nothing but luck for many nights to come." She waved to him good bye.

"And farewell to you, as well, Mistress Ehiztaria." He gave her a slight bow before running off to catch up with his uncle.

"If we go straight to the tailor when we leave, I am certain we can have the necessary clothes made for you by the next meeting," he said, recounting the days in his mind. "We shall also have to pay a visit to the blacksmith in order to get the right weapon for you. Perhaps twin daggers would suit you well..."

"All will be fine, Asher. We have plenty of time to get all the things I will need for my initiation," Paul said, waving it off as no big deal.

"Very well, Paul. If you are not worried, then I shall not worry."

"We will just worry about the tailor today. The blacksmith can wait until morrow."

With that being said, the two returned to the village in silence. The tailor still had his door open and quickly took Paul's measurements and special requests.

"Give me seven days' time to work on such outfits. Though I must warn you, the price will not be low," the tailor stated.

"Money is not an object which we are concerned about. As long as you have it ready when you say it will be ready, you will receive your pay," Asher replied.

"Very well. In seven days' time, they shall be ready. However, if you do not mind staying around a moment longer, I shall at least make the cloak for you now. You do not want to catch a chill during these cool, autumnal days. I have seen one too many come for their cloaks too late..." He was already picking up some black fabric and beginning to sew.

Asher motioned for Paul to take a seat in a chair by the door. "How long will this take you to do, kind sir?" he asked.

"Only half an hour's time," he assured.

"Do you mind if I leave the boy alone with you?"

"Can he pay for it himself?" That was the only thing that ever bothered the tailor.

"Yes. He can pay," he replied, slipping some coins from his bag to Paul.

"Very well. You are free to leave," he said, dismissing him with a wave of his hand.

"You can meet me back at our bed chamber when the man has finished your cloak. I have some personal matters I must attend to in the meantime." He patted the boy on the shoulder before walking out of the tailor shop.

"So, lad, what is the special occasion you will need all of these new clothes for?" the tailor asked as he worked.

"I simply outgrew my old clothes," he said with a shrug of his shoulders. "It does little good to wear clothes that do not fit. You agree, no?"

"Ah, yes. It is terrible to live with such problems, but you do not have to worry about that when you are a tailor, as was your father, his father, and his father's father!" he laughed.

Paul laughed as well, though it was not as sincere as it sounded. He could not care *less* about what this man had to say to him, but it was better to come across as a good guy than to be loathed as an enemy. Friends were easier to stab in the back. Brutus had proved that many years ago when he had killed the trusting Julius Caesar.

"It is a drab existence, I know, but it puts bread on the table and new fabric on the shelves..."

The words continued going in one ear and out the other. This little town would be the perfect place to start his take over. Once he was knight, he would be certain to find a way to become King. After all, Princess Dawn truly seemed to love the human who had once owned this body. He was certain he could keep this love and twist it so that it would prove useful to him.

"And then there was this time my father was asked to make the jester's clothes! Oh, the fabrics that went into that outfit were enough to make any man laugh!"

Why was this man still talking to him? Was he truly that good of a faker, or was this man just desperate for someone to talk to? He was glad when the cloak was finally finished. He paid the man as quickly as he could and left, adorning his new cloak made from fabric that looked as though it had been woven with his very own shadows. It seemed perfectly fitting to the shadow spirit that inhabited the body.

Back at the castle, he found Asher sorting through the old clothes in the trunk. "I do not even know why I still have all of this old junk, anyway. It is not like I shall ever fit into these clothes again!" He tossed aside outfit after outfit that looked as though he had worn them many years ago when he was probably still a page or squire. Certainly he had no need for them. "Come hither, boy! Let me see that new cloak of yours!"

Paul walked over and held up the hem of the cloak, turning around for his uncle. It was a little longer than a normal cloak, but he figured the man wanted it to last him for a long time.

"Ah, yes. The tailor did a splendid job on it! You will look wonderful standing before the leaders of the Orion Clan wearing that. Now all you will need is the rest of your outfit and some suitable weapons. Then, you will be a marvelous Hunter! And to think, your father would have wasted all of this talent had I not gotten to you!" Asher laughed. "But that is enough for tonight. We should hit the hay. Tomorrow is the 'big battle.' You must be well rested if you do not wish to die!"

"Believe you me, Asher, you shall have nothing to worry about come tomorrow. The battle will be over before it even begins," Paul said before curling up in his bed. He yawned as he pulled up the covers. "They will never know what hit them..." Just as he was about to fall asleep, a tiny bundle landed on his lap. "What is this?" he asked, sitting up.

"That is what I really went out to do," he replied, propping himself up on his elbow to watch as the boy began to unwrap the fabric from around the object. "You don't think I really sat there going through that chest the whole time, did you?"

Paul smiled from ear to ear, holding up the gift. They were daggers crafted from pure obsidian with simmering silver hilts that fit perfectly into his hands. "How did you manage to get these made in only a half hour's time?" he asked.

"I had the blacksmith start them this morning before we even arrived at the clan meeting. All that remained was picking them up. You will not be fighting tomorrow, but it helps to be able to fend for yourself just in case," he said with a wink.

Paul put them off to the side with his cloak. "Thank you kindly, Asher. I owe you greatly."

"Just work your hardest and that shall be payment enough." He nodded his head "good night" before curling up under the covers, and Paul did the same. Tomorrow would certainly prove to pay him immensely.

CHAPTER 11

It was not long after the sun began spreading its tendrils of light into the room that the squire awoke. He would need to prepare his master's horse! Quickly, he ran out of the room, only bothering to grab his cloak and daggers from his bedside. When he reached the stables, Asher was already there, feeding his horse a bright orange carrot.

"Oh! There you are, Paul! I was wondering when you would wake! I would have raised you myself, but you looked so peaceful in your sleep," he chuckled, patting his strawberry roan stallion as it chewed on the nub of the carrot.

"But that is one of my duties as a squire, is it not? To tend to your horse?" he asked, wrinkling his brow in confusion.

"You caring for my horse will do nothing to teach you the true meaning of knighthood. It would also give you the wrong opinion of knights, for we are not lazy good for nothings who require others to do all of our work for us," he explained. "Besides, old Furymane here does not like others caring for him. He will not even let the stable hands take care of him, but, hey, it does not bother me. It helps to spend time with your steed. It builds a stronger bond."

Paul nodded and his eye wandered over to Umbra. It seemed as though no one had really been paying much mind to the black stallion that morning. The typical brandishing of a war horse was not present. "Who does Umbra belong to?" he asked.

"No one. He will not let anyone near him. People say he is demon possessed! Ha! They know nothing about the subject!" he chortled.

He laughed with him. *Neither do you, old man,* he thought. "Then why does he let me come near and pet him?"

Asher stopped short. "Umbra lets you near? This I have to see... Go over to yonder horse. Touch its muzzle. Prove to me these things which you say, you bluff!"

Paul shrugged and walked over to the horse. Umbra merely cocked his head to the side and brayed his approval. Slowly, he reached out and brushed the tips of his fingers along the horse's soft head. Still, the horse only neighed.

"Amazing..." Asher mumbled, walking over.

The horse remained calm until Paul left its side. Then, it began to stamp its hooves fiercely, snorting angrily at Asher as though he were warning him to stand back should he value his life. Asher held up his hands to show he meant no harm and backed away. "Well, it looks like we have found your steed!" he said, pushing Paul towards the horse. "Go ahead. Saddle him up. It will do me more good to have you ride beside me than behind on the same horse."

With a nod, Paul walked over to the horse and began taking the tack off the wall next to him so he could properly saddle him. After a glance into the horse's soulful, or rather soulless, eyes, he proceeded to put the saddle and reigns on. The entire time, Umbra was nothing but complacent. He moved in ways that were entirely helpful to the young boy as he saddled up the horse—his horse!—for the first time.

Once Paul completed this task, he mounted as Asher had moments before.

"Here. Carry this for me," Asher said, tossing him a sheathed broadsword. "Just because you are my nephew does not mean I am going to go completely soft on you." He rode out of the stables and Paul followed suit. Once outside, Asher spoke again. "I need to go suit up. Wait for me here, and I shall return in a moment." He passed the reigns off to Paul before running over to the castle.

"Lucky... Why do they even make us bother with this stupid training? I could be fourfold the knight that he is." Paul shook his head. "I would not even have to try! But, no. They make us go through this training and for what? Nothing..."

"It is a great honor to make it to even the position of squire!" his conscience, the original spirit of Paul, told the dark spirit. "One must learn before one can teach! If we went into the battlefield unprepared, who knows what might happen to this world of ours!"

"Shut up, child. This is no longer your body, no longer your mind, no longer your thoughts. Now, stand aside once more and let me have the reigns. This is the dawn of the darkness, of the spirits, of the demons! Your childish thoughts have no place here! Your whims are too human, full of somewhat good intentions! Do not fight what is happening! Your body is mine now, and I shall do as I please, and you shall do nothing to stop me, for there is nothing you can do," the spirit possessing the body rambled on angrily. "Do not resist! You will come to enjoy what is happening, even if you do not realize it as of yet."

Asher walked back. "What in the name of the King are you doing? There is no one here to talk to! Assure me you are not going mad from all of this stress being heaped upon you!" he begged, taking back the reigns.

"All is well, Uncle. I was merely thinking out loud. There were only a few moral questions being brought to mind when I pondered about the battle that will ensue," Paul said with an innocent smile. *Moral questions being brought up by an idiot voice inside my head that does not know when to shut up!* he added in thought. *And that voice better learn else I shall not only instill pain on others!*

He nodded. "Very well. Come. The others are ready to go. We do not want to be responsible for holding them back," he chuckled. He climbed onto the horse, his armour clinking and banging with the movement.

They guided their horses over to the other knights. "What is he doing upon Umbra?" the knight who had been arguing for the broadsword asked.

"A better question is 'how did he get upon Umbra?'" the other knight from the breakfast table corrected.

"Paul is truly special. What else can I say?" Asher asked, nudging his nephew. "Umbra seems to really have taken a liking to him. Was I wrong in allowing him to ride?"

"No. You were correct. He will definitely serve us better this way," the first agreed.

"Sure. Now he can actually serve you rather than hinder you. I cannot even tell you how many times my knight complained that I was getting in the way when I tried to follow him on foot or ride behind him on the horse," the second agreed.

Asher nodded. "Very well. Then, we should be heading out, no? We do not want to give Cahal a large advantage over us," he said, digging his heels into the sides of the horse. "Onward to victory, men!" he cheered.

"For Asthla! For the victory!" the knights chanted as they rode off towards Cahal.

All the while, Paul pondered what was about to go on. He knew for a fact that his father would be there. There was no question about it. What would that mean for him? He could feel that the real Paul was only half approving of his plan to kill his father. After all, his father had completely ostracized him once Ammira was born and, not only that, but he was a rebel! The sentence for rebelling was death, a sentence that had almost been passed down to him without even giving him a chance to fight against it. It was at that thought that he could sense the original boy's true feelings. His father would have traded his life away for nothing and would not even care about it! Only one thought could now pass through his head. Laurence Carson Hunter had to die, or he would die trying!

CHAPTER 12

It was a different world out on the battlefield, a world that was strange and unfamiliar to the young squire. He had heard many tales about what it would be like out there, but he never knew that he would actually experience it the way he was. All around him, there were cries of joy, of anguish, of pride, of pain. It was frightening, yet, at the same time, exhilarating! Asher did not allow him to leave his side, and the two fended off their enemies well together.

All the while, Paul's eyes searched the battlefield for one thing: his good-for-nothing father. He knew that his father would be among the ranks where more Asthlans were dying. Sure enough, in the middle of a ring of dead Asthlans was Laurence, standing tall with another knight of Cahal. It was obvious it was him. He could see how he resembled this man. Now would be the end of any similarity, however.

Paul turned the reigns of his horse and geared it towards his father. The men looked up and prepared for battle, but Laurence recognized his own son and called off the other man. "It is alright, Sir Pedric. He is not an enemy," he stated. "Leave me be so that I might speak with yonder youth alone."

Sir Pedric shrugged his shoulders. "Whatever you say, Sir Laurence. I shall make peace elsewhere." He shifted his mare's reigns and headed off toward a knot of fighting knights to offer his assistance.

Once Paul reached him, he pulled the stallion to a stop. "Ah. So I see you *do* remember me!" he scoffed. "You have not forgotten about me with that new bundle of joy around in your life? I am surprised. You sure fooled me! Did you not care to keep contact with me the past seven years?"

The look on Laurence's face was one of complete and utter pain, though it was not a physical pain. "I am terribly sorry, Paul. I did not forget you, but it is not easy to care for Ammira without her... your... mother."

"There you go again! Nearly forgetting about me!" he hissed, fists clenching in increasing anger.

"Paul! If you would only listen to me! I tried to make contact with you, but you broke the whistle! That was my only contact with you!" he replied, eyes growing increasingly sad.

"So you could not send a letter? Other pages were receiving letters from their fathers who were actually *worried* and *cared* about them, but did I ever receive one from the runner? NO!" His own dark eyes began gleaming, as if there were actually some kind of light coming through them.

"Forgive me, son! You must know that I truly was too busy!"

"TOO BUSY FOR YOUR OWN SON!?! TOO BUSY FOR A SHORT LETTER FOR YOUR OWN SON?!?"

Laurence shrunk back, resembling a kicked puppy. "I am sorry, Paul!"

"Your apologies mean absolutely nothing to me! Nothing at all! Why would you even bother with these idiotic words?" He drew his twin daggers from his pockets.

"Paul? What are you doing? I love you, son! What are you doing!?!" he gasped, tugging the reigns of his horse and pulling it away from his demented son. "Paul! Come to your senses!"

"I have finally come to my senses, Father! And my senses all say that you have not been my father! Uncle Asher is more of a father than you are!" he hissed, jumping off his own horse for easier maneuvering.

"Please do not tell me you have been listening to my brother! That man does not know a thing about raising children!" Laurence gasped, shaking his head. He got off his horse so he could be closer to his son's level, hoping that it would help to appease him.

"And you do? That is not a viable argument on your part!"

Asher could hear the argument from where he was a few hundred yards away and dismounted, running over to see what it was that the two were doing. "Ah... So it is you, brother!" Asher gasped with a smirk. "It has been a long time! Far too long!" He rested a hand on Paul's shoulder, and the boy relaxed slightly though his daggers were still held up at the ready.

"Why have you been poisoning this child's mind? I sent him here to learn the values of knighthood, not hatred!" Laurence scolded.

"Oh, please. You know as well as I do hatred comes with the job!" he laughed. "I am surprised you have not pieced that together by now! But, then again, there are a lot of things that you have yet to figure out." He glanced down at Paul. "The thing that surprises me the most, however, is that you were willing to risk your son's life without even giving him a chance to learn of the benefits of the Orion Clan and the penalties he would flee by joining it."

"Death is better than destruction. I would sooner die than join that blasphemous group," Laurence said, for once gaining venom in his voice.

"Oh, so you would?" Asher chuckled. He released Paul's shoulder. "Go ahead, Paul. Teach your father a lesson he shan't soon forget."

Paul raised one of the daggers, but, just as he was about to bring it down, there was a flicker of color in his eyes, though only a slight hint of the brown that had once been there. "Father..." he mumbled.

"Please, Paul. You do not wish to do this! Do not do it, Paul! Do not listen to your uncle! Listen to me! I am your father!" Laurence begged.

The boy began shaking his head as an inward struggle began between him and the spirit. "I will not kill him!" Paul tried to shout, though his voice came out rather strangled, for, in truth, the spirit was strangling his own former self's conscience in a futile attempt to silence it.

"Paul! Finish the deed! Prove your worth as a Hunter!" Asher demanded.

His hands tightened on the daggers' handles to the point at which his knuckles turned white. He glared at his father, but he couldn't manage to bring himself to finish the deed. He took another look at his uncle and then at his father. Sure, his father was sentenced to death by the Orion Clan, but there had to be something else he could do. His conscience refused to let him actually kill his father, even though it had been the plan all along.

"Perhaps we do not have to kill him. Could we not hold him captive?" Paul asked.

"Paul! What are you saying?" Laurence demanded, obviously holding back tears. "What are you doing, Paul?"

Asher smiled a rather sadistic smile. "Ah... I see what you are saying. That is a far worse punishment for a knight," he laughed. "Tie him up."

Paul nodded. Sir Laurence was far too frightened and confused to run from his son and brother. The two easily tied his arms and legs before dragging him away from the battlefield so they could take him back at a later time. Once they left him in a hidden location, they returned to the battle themselves so as not to raise suspicion.

CHAPTER 13

Not long after the family reunion, the battle drew to a close. The knights from Cahal surrendered to the Asthlans. A few survivors were permitted to return to Cahal to spread the news of their demise while the Asthlans returned to their homes victorious with some of the survivors held prisoner. Among the Asthlans were Asher and Paul. They had survived the battle, though the two knights they had spoken to only that morning did not make it to see the end of the battle and lay rotting on the ground.

Paul was exhilarated when he returned to the stables to take the tack off Umbra. His first battle and, not only had he won, but he had made his first kills! Adrenaline was still pounding through his veins when he saw Princess Dawn watching him from the door to the stables. The knights were busy talking amongst one another, so he slipped outside and around the back of the stable with her.

"Oh, Paul! I fretted you would not return! Yet, here you are, in the living flesh!" she chirped, getting up on her toes and kissing his cheek. "My brave knight!"

"Squire," he corrected her.

"Squire, knight, it matters not! All that matters is that you are alive!" She held his hands tightly in her own, feeling his flighty pulse with her fingertips. "You should relax, Sir Paul!" she teased. "Must I give you another kiss?"

"If I might be so bold," he said, leaning down and kissing her cheek instead.

She giggled and blushed a bright crimson. "Oh, Paul!"

"I love you, Princess Dawn," he whispered. "You know that I do, with every fiber in my body and every ounce of my heart!"

"I love you, too, dear Paul, but our love still cannot be!" She pouted. "Stupid laws... Why can a girl not follow her own heart?"

"I am certain we shall find a way around this obstacle, Princess. We always seem to!" He gave her another kiss, but pulled away quickly. Someone was calling his name. "I must leave you for now!" he apologized. "I will meet you here tonight!"

She smiled and waved with her fingers. "Until then, my *knight*."

He returned her smile and ran off. In truth, the demonic spirit could care less about the Princess, but if he let in on that, it would become obvious to her that something was amiss with him, and she would seek out the truth. Instead, he decided to humor both her and Paul's conscience. After all, what could it hurt? Besides that, this girl would bring him one step closer to the throne.

Paul turned and smiled at his uncle. "Hello, Asher. What is the reason you have called for me?" he asked in an innocent, almost angelic, voice.

"We must go to the King to announce our triumph over the kingdom of Cahal. You shall be expected to be there to speak for the squires of our kingdom since you are one of the few whom survived," Asher stated.

"I thought this was supposed to be a mock war! Why would so many of the younger generations die?" he pondered.

"Not everyone was aware that it was fake. Only you, Sir Pedric, and I knew that it had no true purpose behind it for our kingdoms have not feuded in many years. Some of the men whom had squires among their ranks took the war extremely seriously. As is typical, the knight would die and the squire would try and avenge his master's death, which would lead to his own," he explained.

He nodded curtly. "Very well." With that, they headed back to the castle with the other survivors.

Never before had Paul ventured into this part of the castle. He was used to going only from Sir Ivan's chambers to the stables and occasionally the practice grounds or going from Asher's quarters to these same places, but never to the throne room. It frightened him, though not entirely. He knew that within the throne room, he would once more see his Princess.

The large room was lavished with the finest materials one could buy. The mahogany thrones looked as though they were worth more than the entire royal treasury with their golden inlaid inscriptions and incrusted gems of the finest rubies, sapphires, and emeralds. They greatly resembled the crowns upon the heads of both the King and the Princess.

Along with the knights and squires, there were a few Lords who had served in the battle present. Among them was Lord Ivan Averk who glared coldly at Paul, obviously upset with the fact that the boy did not look as though he had received a proper beating in who knew how long. Paul returned this glare with stone cold eyes that even looked as though they were chiseled out of the stone itself.

There was the blast of a trumpet as the King was announced to speak. He slowly rose from the throne.

"Dear Lords, knights, squires!" the King began, his voice echoing throughout the room. "I see before me the best of the best who have survived against all odds! My praise to you, and my condolences to those of you who have lost dear friends in the day's battle! It was short, yet I see that it took a great toll on our numbers. Nonetheless, that will not affect us! Might the squires take a step forward?"

Paul stepped toward the King, as did a few others who were around his age.

"In but a few years time, these young men will be joining us at the mighty rank of knights! Once more, our numbers shall be great indeed! Tell me, Sir-to-be Paul, how many more summers until you are ready to join our ranks?" he asked, looking down at the boy.

"Five," he answered boldly.

"Ah. Five years! It will not be long! Three for some, two for others! I thank thee all kindly for serving your knights as well as myself. How have you fared during your first battle, Paul?"

"I have fared well, your Majesty. I look forward to not only serving Sir Asher, but fighting by his side!" he replied.

"Splendid, boy! You may return to your quarters now, squires. I wish to speak to the nobles alone." He waved his hand at the squires.

As Paul passed Asher, he could hear his uncle whisper, "Five more summers is shorter than you think!"

He nodded quickly and headed out of the room with the other squires.

One, the eldest, turned to look at him. "Five more years before you can join the knights? I pity you. I will be joining in but a single year so long as I can come up with the money for the suit of armour," he laughed. "What is with you, talking to the King as though you were the most noble of all squires? I bet you cannot fight nearly as well as you can speak!" The other squires joined in the laughter.

"You are unwise to laugh at me," Paul replied. "I could easily kill you, and I would not even have to touch you!"

This made the squires chortle even more boisterously. "Ooh! I am so frightened! That is impossible, lest you be a witch! In that case, perhaps you should be burned at the stake!" the squire continued to jest.

"I have warned you once, and I shall not warn you again. It would be wise if you kept your mouth shut before it gets you into great trouble," he hissed, temper flaring.

"Aw! The tiny boy wants to fight me. Go ahead. Punch me," he said, sticking out his chin to the smaller boy. "Come on, now. Don't be shy. Punch me!"

"If you insist," Paul replied, shrugging his shoulders. He pulled back his fist and snapped it out, making swift contact with the boy's jaw.

He stumbled back a few steps, rubbing it in pain. "Get him!" he hissed at the others, cringing in pain as he did so. "Do not let him escape!"

"That is quite alright. I was just thinking about leaving you be," Paul said with a listless smile. He pulled up his cloak and disappeared into the shadow of the lead boy.

"Where did he go? Find him!" he demanded the other squires. They nodded and dispersed.

The leader, whom was named Arson, began to search around the hall while the others dispersed. The boy had just left, so he could not have gotten far. He lifted up a tapestry and glanced behind it. There was no sight of the boy behind there.

Mischievously, Paul pulled Arson's shadow up from the ground and tapped him with the squire's own shadowy finger before making the shadow and himself quickly fall into hiding behind him.

Arson quickly turned around, fist raised. To his great disappointment, Paul was not there. He growled and continued his search. "Come out of hiding, Paul! Do not hide like a coward in the shadows!" he hissed.

"Then I shall stop hiding," Paul laughed, jumping out of Arson's shadow, this time poking him on the back with his own finger. "Boo!"

Arson turned around once more and quickly hurled a punch which Paul easily dodged under. "Stand still, you little pest!" he growled, trying once more. Again, he failed.

"That is quite alright, sir. I value my life, though yours, I value not," he said, scooping up the squire's shadow as though it were an actual, tangible thing and not only a mere play of light. "Farewell, Arson." He swiftly wrapped it around Arson's neck.

"What are you do-" he began, but never got to finish his sentence. His eyes bulged in surprise as he could actually feel the shadow tightening around his neck, squeezing out every breath he had in his body and preventing him from grabbing new ones. He gasped frantically, but to no avail. Slowly, the life was sucked out of his body and he lay on the ground, motionless, at Paul's feet.

"Such a clean method of disposing of such a nuisance as you, Arson," he scoffed, dragging him out of the castle by the shadow around his neck. He took him all the way to the woods, unnoticed by any human eye, and left the body with its shadow beneath a tree. "This does not look believable..." he mumbled, looking down at the obviously strangled boy. He snapped his fingers as an idea popped into his mind.

Within moments, he had woven a rope from the flexible branches of a nearby weeping willow and tied it as a noose around the squire's neck. "Now that is believable," he said, leaving the body and returning to the castle.

Night was quickly approaching, as was his time alone with Princess Dawn. This was certainly something he could look forward to. The acting that he put into their meetings gave him a sick kind of joy, but it was not in the acting itself. The more he met with Princess Dawn, the more believable to her, and quite possibly to others, and the more he seemed to be like the original Paul who had not so long ago been exiled from this body's control. Soon, he would no longer even worry about others believing he had changed. This was what he looked forward to, and this was what he aimed for.

As he returned to the castle, he whistled the merry tune he had sung when he first met the boy. There was a gaiety in his step as he continued to whistle before he began to sing the short song to himself.

CHAPTER 14

Sure enough, the night was upon them. Asher had turned in for the night rather early, but Paul told him that he would like to go for a walk. His uncle merely nodded in agreement before he fell asleep. Paul slipped outside, unawares to anyone but his uncle and Princess Dawn.

The world looked so much different when he was out at night. His vision was keen, picking up even the minutest details, be it a blade of grass or a tiny worm coming out of the ground. Never before had his sight been so perfect. He amused himself with a baby spider spinning its first web. The tiny creature fumbled a few times but nevertheless managed to make a beautiful web.

He turned his attention away from the spider and headed off to the barn. Though the moon's light did not offer him to see in the vast array of colors he could see in during the day time, the grays were still just as contrasting as the vibrant greens and blues. The rather light gray of the grass was broken by the darker gray of the looming barn. He smiled for he knew that beyond this vast blob of gray stood his "love." He could already see her in his mind, standing there and looking to and fro frantically, pondering where it was that her dear Paul could be. Not wanting to make her wait any longer, he stepped around the back of the barn.

"Oh, Paul!" she chirped, running up to him and throwing her arms around his neck. "You came! You came! I was beginning to think you had forgotten!"

"I had to wait for my uncle to meet sleep. If I were to leave while he was still awake, he might try and find out where it is that I should venture off to so late at night. When he is half asleep, however, he is very easy going," he laughed.

"It matters not! What matters is that you are here with me now!" She dared yet another kiss upon his cheek. "Come, Paul! I must show you a secret!" She grabbed his hand and drug him out to the forest.

Paul chewed on his lip, hoping that they would not stumble across Arson's body. His keen eyes could make out the body a few yards to his left, but Princess Dawn was too preoccupied with finding her "secret." He breathed a sigh of relief when the body escaped even his eye sight.

He had thought that being outside the castle in the dark was like a different world. The forest itself, in contrast, seemed like a completely different universe. Looking around the forest, he could see every leaf, even more distinct than ever. Every branch seemed like an arm, waving to him a friendly hello. Even the little ticks on the ground seemed to be watching him and saying hello as they pondered whether or not to jump upon his leg and drink of his blood.

Princess Dawn did not appear to be as fazed by this sudden transformation of the woods as he was, though he figured that she was not in touch with the shadows like he was. He did not mind this, however, for this would be *his* little secret and his hiding place.

Finally, Princess Dawn ceased her stumbling through the forest and stopped in front of a tiny babbling brook. "We are here!" she announced, sitting down next to the water and pulling him down with her. "This is my own secret brook! It tells me bedtime stories every night!" She lay down and touched her hand upon the water's surface. The ripples appeared to almost spell out "greetings" in response to her.

"It is beautiful. Is it telling you a story right now?" he asked, leaning closer.

She nodded. "It is, indeed. It is telling me a story of two lovers whose love could not be!"

"I cannot understand the brook's language. Would you like to tell it to me?"

She beamed from ear to ear. "Okay!" She moved closer to the water and listened intently.

"There once was a knight who clad himself in the finest armour made of gold. He went by the name of Victor, for he could never be defeated in battle, though his real name was Paul." She paused and winked. "Every night, Victor would return from his various battles and meet the stunningly beautiful Princess Dawnella, whom everyone referred to as Dawn." She laced her fingers with his at this point.

"One day, Victor returned from his latest battle: defeating the mighty gorgon, offspring of Medusa, with her serpentine hair! He went to the place where Dawn had always met him, but the Princess was not there. Victor was not alarmed, for there had been many days when he had been late to their meetings, so he waited for her. He continued to wait until the sun stretched over the horizon. This frightened him.

"He returned to the castle to seek out her father. The only thing her father knew was that she had left in the middle of the night to go for a walk as she always did. This frightened him even more, so he returned to the forest and checked every inch of the woods for his Princess Dawnella! Sadly, his Dawnella was nowhere to be seen.

"Disheartened, Victor left the kingdom and traveled to a neighboring one that was surrounded by vast mountains. While he was passing the base of the mighty mountain range, he could hear a shrill voice screaming from its precipice! It belonged to none other than Dawnella! He climbed the mountain with such speed! It was almost as though he was being borne up on the wings of an eagle.

"Before an hour's time had passed, he found his Princess Dawnella chained to a rock at the feet of a mighty beast! A large black dragon whose snout alone was the size of Victor! This did not bother Victor in the least.

"'Unhand my Princess, foul beast!' Victor shouted at the creature." Here, she mimicked Paul's voice, rather deep.

"'Never, mortal! She shall be my feast!' the dragon replied." She made her voice go even deeper and growled slightly as she spoke for the dragon.

"'I refuse to leave this mountain without her!'

"'Then you shall also become a part of my dinner!'

"Undaunted, though greatly angered, Victor lunged toward the dragon, his mighty broadsword held high. It pierced through the dragon's soft underbelly with ease, sending blood spurting forth.

"With the dragon out of the way, Victor returned to the Princess and used his sword to slice through the chains that bound her. As soon as she was free, she rewarded her hero with a kiss." She paused her story and kissed Paul once more. "When the two returned to their village, hand in hand, the King held a splendid feast and the two were married that very night. And they lived happily ever after as King and Queen. The end." She bowed her head.

Paul clapped his hands quickly. "That was a beautiful story. And the brook has told you this?" he asked.

She blushed. "Maybe..." She smiled shyly at him.

"Well, tell the *brook* that it has told a wonderful story," he laughed. He could feel Paul's conscience screaming to let him take control, to hug the Princess close. He wanted so badly to make the story a reality, though only the ending that resulted in their marriage.

"Do not speak another word. Let only our hearts talk to one another," she whispered. She rested her head upon his chest and closed her eyes.

Paul smiled to himself. Even evil spirits liked love sometimes. He chuckled quietly to himself and patted the girl's soft hair. It was obvious to him that she had fallen asleep, so he stopped moving and let her rest, though he himself had far too much on his mind to actually fall asleep.

He watched as her chest moved slightly up and down as she dreamed. This brought some joy to him. He was certain that now she would never question whether or not he was Paul. That was a good thing, for if she backed him up, so would everyone else. There was no questioning the authority of the Princess. Her word meant almost as much as her father's.

He had not realized until now how much this girl had grown over the past years. When he came, she was no more than a child, as was he. Now, she looked like a true woman. He longed so much to marry her, to claim her as his own. The spirit was not strong enough to keep out all of the conscience's affections. It was no longer just a mere want for power, but a want for her.

While he got lost in the thoughts of his fantasies, he could see the moon nearly reaching the end of its rounds. Gently, he shook Princess Dawn's shoulder. "Awake, my Princess! Dawn is soon approaching, dear Dawn! We must return to our chambers."

Dawn yawned and stretched her frail arms. "Already?" She stuck out her lower lip. "We should make like the people in our stories and meet here every night. Will you do that for me, Paul? Will you come and meet me?" she asked as the two began to get up.

"Yes, Princess Dawn. I promise that I shall come and meet you here every night for as long as we two shall live," he promised.

She smiled. "Thank you, Paul! This shall be most joyous! Oh, thank you!" She gave him one more kiss before they departed from the dark forest that would forever hold their secret. "I must be the luckiest girl in the world."

"And I must be the luckiest boy, for I have such a lucky girl to love me," he replied before they broke free of the forest's veil.

CHAPTER 15

Paul trudged back into Asher's quarters and lay down on the bed. After staying up all night, he greatly looked forward to the rest and relaxation. He curled up under the covers and closed his eyes. No sooner did he begin to feel the first wave of calming relaxation rush over him, he felt something shaking his shoulder.

"Get up, Paul! No time to rest right now!" whatever was shaking him called out to him. "Get up! Now, Paul!"

With a groan, the boy waved it off.

"Right now, Paul!" Now the thing began to shake him even harder.

"I'm up, I'm up..." Paul groaned, sitting up in the bed and rubbing the sleep from his eyes. He looked up at his Uncle Asher. "Why must we wake so early?"

"It is no earlier than we have ever woken before," he laughed. "Come on, Paul! Look alive! After all, we have to go visit our prisoner!"

"Did we not leave him by the battlefield?" he asked, still trying to wake up.

"While you were out on your walk, wherever you went on that-" he paused and raised an eyebrow, "-I returned to the battlefield and picked him up. He had been trying to run away, but he did not make it very far with his arms and legs bound. That man is full of so much hot air! He is all talk, but no action." He shook his head as he chuckled to himself. "Any matter, you should come. I believe you two should have another chance to talk, do you not?"

The last bit of sleep was wiped from his eyes. "So he is in the dungeon?" He smirked. "Oh, how grand. I wonder how he likes the feeling of being taken from home and tormented daily as I had been."

"Come now, child," he said, beckoning to him to follow as he left the room. This was yet another unexplored part of the castle to Paul.

As they descended the stairs to the dungeons, Paul could feel a heightening in his senses once more as he had when he had gone into the forest at night. The room was very dark; a regular human would barely be able to see his own hand in front of his face. There were places, however, where anyone could see, but that was only in the light of the torches.

There were various rooms with different people within them, moaning and motioning to the two as they passed, hoping that one would reach out a helping hand and free them from this torment. This brought a smile to Paul's lips. Such death and despair was what the spirit had grown to enjoy all of the years that he himself felt that same despair.

Once they had passed these rooms, there were other chambers which had their doors open to reveal torture chambers and the executioner's rooms. He noticed one room had various whips while another contained little more than a wooden block and a blood stained battle ax. The spirits emanating from these rooms were immense due to the many that had before died in them. Perhaps his father's own spiritual being would be added to these tormented souls in due time.

After these rooms, Paul could see only one figure in the shadows, its wrists chained just above its head. Unlike all of the others within this prison, it was not moaning. Rather, it appeared as though whoever it was was sobbing loudly, their face turned so that none who entered could see who he was.

Paul approached this person, moving to their other side so that he might see who it truly was. "Ah, how the mighty have fallen," he laughed, finally observing the man's face.

"How could you, Paul? How? This is not like the little boy I had raised you as! Why, Paul? Why?" Laurence cried out to his son as he looked into his son's soulless eyes.

"And how could you send me off to live with Lord Ivan Averk? What kind of a father sends away his son to a place where he is tormented daily? Huh? Can you answer that for me, *Father*?" he hissed. "And the last news you ever gave to me was the news of Mother's death! What kind of father tells their child that and then never talks to them again? I knew there was a reason I loved Mother more than you!" He knew that that was below the belt, but that was what he aimed for.

Laurence continued to sob as he peered into the face of the child. "Who are you now, Paul? You certainly are not the same child I sent here. Who has changed you as such?"

"No one has changed me. I have changed myself." There was certainly more behind that saying than what the average person would get out of it. "And you know what, Father? This change is for the better! The Paul that you wanted me to be is not the Paul that I should have become! That is not me! It never will be me! So just get over it, Father!" His hand balled up into a fist and quickly snapped out, hitting his father square in the jaw.

Sir Laurence cringed. "How, Paul? Why, Paul? When, Paul? Who, Paul?" he sputtered.

"This is not a trial! The answers to your questions mean nothing because there are no answers to your questions."

Fretting what might verbally ensue that could threaten their plan, Asher stepped in and stood between the two, holding his hands up to hold back Paul. "Calm, Paul. Calm is the best way to handle these situations. You cannot let this all go straight to your head and come out in an outburst of anger!" he said soothingly.

With a snarl, Paul punched at the wall beside his father, not even cringing when he made contact and his knuckles were sliced open on the rough, uneven surface of the stone. "I am through here! Farewell, Father. Enjoy rotting in the dungeons! Perhaps I shall remember you as you never did me," he scoffed before turning and storming out of the castle.

He passed the guards as he exited. They began to raise questions, but a single look from him warned them otherwise. He ceased his running when he reached the stable at which point he hopped onto Umbra without bothering to put on his saddle or reigns. With one hit from his heels, the horse flew from its stall and galloped off at top speed.

It was a futile hope that the rushing air would give him time to clear his brain. After all these years, here was his father and right in his very grasp! Yet it seemed that his father had never been so far away before. There was a vast canyon betwixt them, and neither one could find a way to build a bridge or leap across it without falling down and having to climb back up. Right now, Sir Laurence was at the bottom of that canyon, and Paul had no thoughts of helping him to once more rise out of it. Rather he would throw boulders down and laugh whenever Sir Laurence's climb was hindered by him.

The ride was beginning to prove to only escalate his emotions. This was the tiny piece of conscience that was ever present in this body, the only remnant of the original Paul. There was always this little bit within him that still loved his father and wanted all to end well, yet it knew that nothing could ever be the same between them. It was this miniscule part that longed to jump down into the canyon with Sir Laurence and just stay there with him in a world where they would both be wrong, yet they would at least be wrong together. This was the conscience's dream, but it was not the spirit's.

The spirit wished to keep Sir Laurence as far away as possible, especially if that meant that his father would be spending an excess amount of time at rock bottom, just barely making his way through life. He would forever hold him down and keep him from meeting him at any point and also from rising back up to full power. With the death of Maria, he was already barricaded from the upper most level of his side of the canyon. It was as though her death had placed spikes in the stone just below the top so that every time he tried to climb, he was forced to stop.

Yet at the top of the canyon on Sir Laurence's side sat a little girl, the young Ammira. She was oblivious to all that was happening, simply waiting for her father to come and meet her. This child, though he could not put a distinct look to her face, was nearly the exact reincarnation of Maria in his mind. Whenever Laurence would near the top, she would hold out her tiny hand and offer to pull him up over the spikes, but her resemblance to Maria was far too close, and he would be distracted by his depression and once more fall to the bottom.

With so many thoughts upon his mind, it was growing increasingly painful to think. What was it? What was it that kept the two from ever meeting? That was when he realized another piece was added to the canyon puzzle.

Standing just below Paul was his white haired uncle, watching him. Beside him was not the conscience of Paul, but the spirit within him. Every time Paul would try and fling himself down to be with his father, they were there, catching him and throwing him back up with their promises and encouragement. They were the ones who truly separated them. It was not that Paul would not fall to be with his father; it was that he could not fall.

The spirit merely rolled his eyes at this conclusion. To him, it meant nothing. Sir Laurence was no longer his father. After all, Asher had been more of a father to him than Laurence had ever been. With this in mind, he completely abandoned the thoughts of the conscience, refusing to listen to another word of it. Not only was it a load of garbage that his conscience was trying to heap on, but it was also not helping him to gain the calm that he was searching for.

With a sigh that mixed slightly with a growl, he rode on, trying to leave behind all of the hurt and deception of the castle life. That was when he found his source of relief! The Princess was out for a ride with the King. Perhaps he could gain some time alone with her. "Hail the mighty King and his glorious daughter!" he called out to them.

The two pulled their horses to a stop and turned to look at who it was that had addressed them as such. "Ah, young squire Paul, what brings you here?" the King asked. Meanwhile, Princess Dawn looked at him with a smile, winking at him.

"I was on a ride while my dear knight, Sir Asher, stayed in the castle to tend to some business. I did not expect to run into the two of you here. If I am intruding, I am terribly sorry," he sighed, tugging on the horse's mane so that he would be heading back to the castle.

"Oh, Father! Can Paul not ride with us? We are not on business!" Princess Dawn pleaded, her eyes playing his heartstrings like a lute.

"Very well. If you so wish it, Princess Dawn," the King said, turning back to Paul. "Come hither, boy! Ride with us a while!"

Paul smiled broadly. "Oh, thank you, sire!" he said, turning Umbra back towards them. He fell into pace beside the Princess. "Good morning, your highness," he said, bowing as best he could while upon a horse's back. He turned and bowed to the King as well.

"Good morning, sir to be Paul," Princess Dawn said with a grin. There was a hint of a blush upon her cheeks.

"How has your training been going, Paul?" the King asked. "Of all of the squires we have ever had come through here, you seem to be quite unlike the rest. Is it that Sir Asher is such a grand teacher?"

"Indeed, Sir Asher is a wonderful teacher who knows very much about training a young squire as myself. Why? Does that surprise you?" he asked.

"Oh, none in the least! Every time our kingdom has seen a descendent of the Hunter family, we can quickly tell. There is a certain skill they possess that none other could ever have. I am beginning to see that in you, Paul. You shall make a wonderful knight, and we will be honored to have you protect our kingdom alongside the other knights," he said, nodding to the boy. "Although by that time, you shall be protecting my daughter, the Queen Dawn, for she shall be marrying in the coming years."

"Father, I have told you that I do not wish to marry any Princes. They do not love me," Princess Dawn objected. "I want to marry for love!"

"I am sorry, Princess Dawn, but the law states that you will wed the one to whom you are betrothed. Unfortunately, we failed to make arrangements for you when you were but a babe, so we shall have to find the proper Prince for you in a different fashion. Nonetheless, you shall marry a Prince," the King replied.

"With all due respect, your majesty," Paul interjected, "I would have to agree with Princess Dawn. The relationship between husband and wife should not be a forced thing.

The Princess should be able to marry whomever she wishes."

"Preposterous, child. What do you even know of the subject? You yourself are just coming of the age of marriage. There is no possible way that you can know what is the best," the King laughed. "If you wish to continue your ride with us, it would be wise if you did not speak of such things as you are currently speaking of."

Paul nodded and bowed his head. "Terribly sorry, Sir," he mumbled. "Perhaps it would be for the better if I did leave..." He tugged the horse's mane and turned it around.

"Please, Paul! Do not leave! Stay a while!" Princess Dawn protested.

"I am sorry, Princess Dawn. Farewell, your majesties." He kicked Umbra's sides and took off back into the forest, wanting to create as much distance between himself and the Princess until night when they could hide together once more in the darkness of the forest at night. The meeting had proved to be a huge mistake, for now he was positive that he and Princess Dawn could never again be united.

CHAPTER 16

Once the sun sank below the horizon, Paul came out of his hiding place within the stables and trudged into the forest. He pulled up the hood of his cloak and disappeared into the shadows of the forest, moving his own shadowy figure from one tree's darkness to the next. There was no joy in this place as there had been. It only brought back the memories of the failed meeting with the King. He knew now that the King would surely hate him for what he had said.

When he came to the river, he stopped. Princess Dawn was already there, though she was not awaiting him anxiously. She was curled up by the side of the brook, her head buried in her hands as she cried. Her whole body shook with each racking sob.

Paul pulled down the hood of his cloak and removed it, laying it over top his crying friend. "Tell me, Princess. What is it that ails you so?" he asked, rubbing her back slowly.

"Father has already begun to send out notices to nearby kingdoms with eligible Princes to come forth to meet me and, he hopes, to ask for my hand in marriage! Oh, Paul! I cannot love any of them! My heart belongs solely to you! I could never give it away to some other man who wishes to have it only so that he may rule another land and use me to have many heirs! I just cannot do it, Paul! That is not the life I want!" she wailed, turning so she could wrap her arms around his neck. "You would never use me as such, Paul! I know it in my heart. Do not let me go to those foul men!"

"I will do my best to help you, Princess Dawn. I will not let your heart be wasted upon such a terrible person," he whispered, lying down beside her. "Here... Rest your head upon my chest and sleep. Do not think of the curses that this world wishes upon you."

Still crying, the Princess lay there with him, her head on his chest as he had asked. She looked up at him, her eyes puffy from so much crying. "Why, Paul? Why can we not be together? I love you, Paul! Why can Father not let me marry such a kind man, even if he were to be but a simple knight? Why is it not like the tales the minstrels sing of where the Princess gives her hand in marriage to her knight in shining armour? Why?" She nestled down and closed her eyes. "Why, Paul? Why?"

"Because this is reality..." he mumbled. "And reality is a terrible place to live..." He shook his head and wiped away her tears with his thumb. "Please. Do not think about it. Rest a while and think of only happy thoughts..." He gently kissed the top of her head.

The song his mother used to sing to him came back into his mind, and as he held Princess Dawn close, he began to whisper the words to her:

"The sun will not rise
If it never set at all.
You'll never know how it feels to heal
If you never first felt pain.
So just close your eyes

85

And rest a while.
The sun will not rise
If it never set at all.
There would be no light
If we never knew of darkness.
There would be no joy
If we never knew of sorrow.
There would be no love
If we never knew of hate.
So just close your eyes
And rest a while.
The sun will not rise,
If it never set at all."

Before Paul could even finish the song, his own eyes grew heavy from fatigue, and he, too, fell into a deep sleep, unlike the night before which he had spent watching over the Princess. It was so deep, that he did not even awaken when something, or someone, removed a screaming Princess Dawn from his side. Even through this, the boy continued to sleep.

CHAPTER 17

When the sun returned to enlighten the sky once more, Paul finally awoke. "Good morning, Princess Dawn," he mumbled, looking down. To his surprise, she was not there. "Oh, Princess?" he called out, looking at the brook. There was still no sign of her. "Ah, well. Perhaps she has returned to the castle."

He walked back to his home quietly, not wanting to draw any attention toward himself. Once in his bed chambers, he saw Sir Asher, sitting on the edge of the bed staring at the floor.

At the sound of footsteps, he looked up. "There you are..." he grumbled, getting up off the bed. Without another word to him, he walked past.

"What is wrong?" he asked, though his uncle did not answer as he stalked down the hallway.

With a shrug, Paul walked over to his own bed. There was a note upon it. He picked it up and read:

Dear Paul,

We know what you have been up to in the woods at night. You would be wise if you ceased your little visits. Or else...

Paul reread the note many times. Who had this come from? Surely it was nothing more than a practical joke. He crumpled it up and tossed it into the fireplace where he would later burn it. Such a silly note. He decided to walk down toward the throne room to see if he could find Princess Dawn.

As he walked by the nurse maid's room, he could hear talking from within. Quietly, he walked over the door to listen in, for he was certain he had heard the name Dawn brought up in the conversation.

"We do not know what happened!" the King said frantically. "I woke this morning to find her in her bed, unconscious by a blow to the head."

"Calm yourself, oh King. I am certain all is going to be fine with her. Just leave her here a while. Within moments, she should wake up. It cannot be anything serious. There are no breaks and no blood," the nurse assured him.

Paul's jaw dropped. The Princess was wounded last night? That must have been why she was not there! He shook his head. Who would do such a thing to Princess Dawn? Who on Earth would have the nerve! As he pondered this, he heard footsteps and disappeared into a nearby shadow.

The King walked out alone, shaking his head. "Oh, my baby... My poor baby girl..." he mumbled to himself as he walked past the shadow upon the wall. He paid no attention to it.

Curiosity burned within Paul, so he slipped into the shadow of the door and peered inside the room. Princess Dawn was lying on a cot, looking as beautiful and peaceful as ever, save the bump on her forehead above her left eye, but even that was not repulsive to the love-struck boy. As he continued to watch, the girl's eyes fluttered open.

"Where am I?" she whispered, slowly turning her head toward the nurse.

"Ah! You are awake once more! What is your name? Do tell," the nurse encouraged.

"Do you not recognize me, dear nurse, as the little Dawn whom you have raised up from infancy? Please tell me. Why does my head hurt so much?" she asked, rubbing the bump on her head. "What happened to me last night?"

"No one knows. Someone came into the castle and must have hit you. But fret not, child. You are fine. Can you get up?"

She hesitantly sat up and swung her legs over the side of the cot. She tottered a bit, like an infant just learning how to walk, but managed to stay upon her feet. "I shall be fine, indeed. Let me go for a walk." She headed out the door.

After checking to see if anyone was in the hall, Paul materialized out of the shadow behind the Princess. "Oh, Princess Dawn!" he gasped, pulling her into a hug. "I am terribly sorry! I should not have fallen asleep! Then I could have prevented this terrible deed from happening! It is all my fault. Please, do forgive me!" he begged.

"It is not your fault, Paul. I do not expect you to stay up all night and then work all day. I am sure it shall never happen again. Perhaps we should wait a while, though, before we continue our meetings in the forest," she said.

He nodded. "There must have been a passing thief. It is fortunate that we are at least still alive. We shall wait a week and then meet again. Though there is one night that I must apologize in advance for, for I have obligations that night."

"Very well, Paul. A week from tonight, I shall once more meet with you in the dark wood. Farewell, Paul. I must find my Father and assure him that I am fine." She pecked him with a kiss before ambling down the hall in search of the King.

"Farewell, Princess Dawn..." he sighed, walking off to his own bed chambers. It was obvious now as to why Asher had been so distraught. Any knight would be if their Princess was hurt and was not properly protected.

CHAPTER 18

The days flew by. Princess Dawn had once more begun to meet with Paul by their secret brook, and they were not bothered again. The boy's new clothes had been tailored and were ready for pick up just as the tailor had said, and it was already time for the coronation ceremony.

Before night could fall, Paul met with Princess Dawn behind the stables. "I must go out tonight with my uncle for some special training. I promise I shall be back tomorrow, and we will once more be able to meet in our secret hideaway. But for tonight, I must go off and leave you here," he said with great regret.

"Worry not, dear Paul. I shall await your return with open arms. Until you return, my knight in shining armour!" She gently kissed his brow. "Farewell!"

"And to my beloved Princess, farewell," he whispered in response, giving her a quick peck on the cheek before running around to the other side of the stable where he met his uncle.

"Are you ready to join our ranks?" Asher asked.

Paul nodded eagerly.

"Do you have your horn? Daggers? Fresh clothes? Cloak? Horse ready?" he continued to question, ticking off all of the things that would be necessary.

"Yes, yes, yes, yes, and *yes*, Uncle Asher. Now, please, let us leave so we are not late!" Paul said, heading into the stable to let Umbra out.

"Very well, Paul. You cannot even begin to fathom how proud of you I am! It is a great honor to become a true Hunter!" Asher cheered, getting atop his own steed.

"Yes, Uncle. You have told me that many times," he sighed.

"And I shall keep telling you, for it is true!" He pulled on the reigns and sent his horse running off into the forest.

Likewise, Paul followed. He had no clue what was in store for him tonight, but no matter what it was, he still looked forward to it.

Once within the forest, Paul began to feel that excitement he would feel when among the shadows. The full moon cast brilliant tendrils of darkness from each tree. This told him that things would certainly go well at his coronation into the Hunters. After all, when he was surrounded by his subjects, how could a shade not have a wonderful time?

They came across a large bonfire which was to be the sight of the assembly. Mistress Ehiztaria was already there, along with some others from the group. She smiled as she watched the two approach. "Ah," she sighed with a smile. "Look who it is? The great Sir Asher and the young Paul! Come, come! All are here but you!" She beckoned to them.

"Asher... Where is everyone else?" Paul asked, noting that only half of the original group was present.

"This occasion is open only to those members who have been through the coronation process themselves. The other members are just ones who come, but they do not actually have membership as these people do and as you will in but a few moments," Asher answered. He moved to stand with the other members but motioned for Paul to go and stand by Mistress Ehiztaria.

She held out her hand to the boy and beckoned him to draw near. "Night has fallen. We have until the moon is at its highest point. Here... Lay down your prize from your first hunt and your weapons," she said, motioning to a stump beside the bonfire.

He nodded and did as he was instructed, placing down the horn and twin daggers of obsidian.

"Marvelous... Such wonderful things for a young member of the Orion Clan to have..." She rearranged the items so that the horn stood up with the daggers leaning against it. Once that was done, she turned to address the crowd. "Let the ceremony begin!" she shouted, holding up her hands.

The group fell silent and watched her with increasing interest. The moon was slowly advancing through the sky, nearing the peak of its rotation.

"Fellow Hunters! We gather here on this night to observe as Paul Carson Hunter joins into our rankings! Behold! Orion has marked the boy's hand himself!" She held up Paul's right hand so that all might see the three markings on the back of it. "And now, we call upon Orion himself to give us his watchful eye!"

As she spoke this, a group of stars in the sky lit up. Brightest of all were the three stars that matched the marking of all Orion Clan members. The crowd watched in awe, having not seen such a thing in many years.

"With Orion watching over us, we give up this boy, Paul Carson Hunter, to be forever one with him! To have his wisdom, to have his knowledge, to have his strength!" she continued.

Paul listened and watched in amazement. Never before had he witnessed anything that was quite like this ceremony. That was, he was amazed until Mistress Ehiztaria tightened her hand around his wrist.

Without another word, she lifted up one of Paul's own daggers and placed its tip upon his hand on the first marking. Slowly, she pressed harder and harder until she drew blood from the mark. Likewise, she drew blood from the other two. This caused Paul to cringe. What was she thinking?

Once that was done, she took the horn from the stump and rested it atop the boy's hand so that a spiral touched each of the marks. The horn slowly became bloody.

"Now, with his blood and his prize, might he become one of us!" she declared, hurling the horn into the bonfire.

A cheer arose from the crowd. They had gained yet another member!

Paul watched the horn slowly burn in the heat of the flames and continued to watch as the black smoke reached up toward the full moon, now high over head. That was his prize! Why would they burn it? He shook his head and looked down at his bleeding hand. What kind of ceremony was this?

Mistress Ehiztaria gave Paul a hug and then proceeded to kiss him on both of his cheeks. "Congratulations, Paul," she said, passing him a rag for his hand.

He smiled slightly. "Thank you, Mistress Ehiztaria. I shall serve you well," he said, bowing his head to her. He wrapped the cloth around his wound.

Sir Asher walked over to him and placed a hand upon his shoulder. "Well, well, well! Look at you! Finally a member of the Orion Clan, eh?" he asked, patting him on the back. "Your father would be so very upset!" he scoffed.

With a smirk, Paul joined in on his laughter. *Take that, Father,* he thought. *I am a part of the Clan, and they actually appreciate and pay attention to me, unlike you!* "We should really head home, Uncle. It would be a great misfortune should we fall asleep on duty," he finally said.

His uncle nodded. "Aye... That could end badly. Good night, Mistress Ehiztaria. We shall see you at the next meeting," he said, bowing his head to their leader.

"Good night, Sir Asher, Paul," she replied, lowering her head slightly. "Farewell! May Orion shine down upon you!"

"And may he also shine down upon you," Asher replied before taking Paul to his horse.

"Why did she stab me and then burn the horn?" Paul asked as he tucked his twin daggers into his cloak.

"It was an offering to Orion so that he might know who you are and that you are worthy. You are just lucky that you were born with the mark of Orion," he laughed.

"Oh? How is that so?" Paul asked, raising an eyebrow.

"If one is not born with our mark yet wishes to join, they must first have the markings branded onto their skin. Then they have their blood drawn from the burn marks. It is a rather painful process," he said, shuddering at the mere thought.

He shook his head. "It seems a bit extreme..." he mumbled.

"It may seem that way at first, but if you think about it, it really is not. The mark allows us to find other members of the Clan," he explained.

"I see..." He continued to think about it. "How can they tell a true member from a false member?"

"You really cannot unless you know of the person's true behavior. For though your father bears the mark upon his shoulder, those who knew him would know that he would never bring harm to a creature of the magical world."

He nodded and rested his head on the top of Umbra's. "That makes sense..." His eyes flitted, half open, half closed.

"Rest for now, Paul. We can speak more in the morning." Before the sentence could even be completed, Paul had nodded off to sleep.

CHAPTER 19

The years flew by, and Paul continued to grow as a man. He was now eighteen, and his new suit of armour was polished and shimmering brightly as he walked through the crowd in the King's throne room. Finally, he was no longer just a squire, but a knight, forever to be known as Sir Paul. He smiled broadly and greeted his fellow knights. His hand rested on the shining ruby pommel of the sword his uncle had given him as a gift since Paul had earned the money to pay for the actual suit of armour.

Once he was through conversing with the knights and his uncle, he slipped outside and found Princess Dawn waiting for him. She was still Princess for her father had as of yet failed to find her a proper suitor. This bothered neither Sir Paul nor Princess Dawn in the least. That afforded them more time to kindle their own love.

"Now I truly can call you Sir Paul," she giggled, pulling him to the side of the castle wall and kissing him upon his lips. "And now you are my knight in shining armour!" She ran her hands down the breast plate, going over the wyvern that was the symbol of Asthla.

He chuckled and ran his hand through her hair. "Indeed you can! And I can still call you my Princess Dawn," he laughed, pulling her into a firm hug. "Perhaps soon we can find a way to make our love a reality. It has been known for a knight to marry a Princess."

"But I know that my father is one to be old fashioned. He will accept nothing less than a Prince of a nearby kingdom whom he can make a treaty with and form an alliance between so that our kingdom might grow! It just isn't fair, Sir Paul! I should be allowed to follow my heart! My father knows not what he is doing! Oh, Paul! What can we d-" She was cut off as Paul kissed her upon her lips to silence her. As he pulled back, she smiled. "Thank you, Sir Paul," she whispered, resting her head on his shining armour.

"But of course, my Princess. We shall find a way to make this work. Love will always find a way," he replied. Even the demonic spirit was beginning to believe that himself. After spending so much time with her, he became absolutely certain that it was not only the boy's conscience that had loved her, but he as well. "There will be a time one day when we can be united as husband and wife and rule the kingdom together, but that day may not come as soon as we hope it would."

"It still does not seem fair that we should have to wait," she continued to pout.

"Please, Princess Dawn. Do not worry about it. Think of the here and now that we share," he whispered, running his hand down her arm slowly. "Just be calm. All is well that ends well, my dear. We know that this will indeed end well." He leaned forward and kissed her again but pulled away quickly. "Someone is approaching!" he hissed.

"Congratulations, Sir Paul!" Princess Dawn cheered in a fake half-caring voice.

"Why, thank you, Princess Dawn," he said, bowing deeply to her.

"Do arise, good knight. Look! Here comes your former master, Sir Asher! Greetings, kind Sir!" she called over to the man behind Paul.

Sir Asher bowed. "Good day, your Highness," he said before straightening. "If you would not mind, Sir Paul has matters to attend to elsewhere. Might I borrow him for the rest of the day?"

"But, of course, Sir Asher!" She nodded her head to Sir Paul. "You may take your leave. Farewell!" she told him.

"Farewell, my Princess," he replied with a slight bow before walking off with his uncle. "Where are we going now, Uncle?" he asked, looking around them to see who else would be in their company. It seemed to be just them.

"Why, to tell Mistress Ehiztaria the glorious news! It is always a great help to the Orion Clan when our members join into the knighthood for it builds both a stronger body and mind. Would you not agree, *Sir* Paul?" he asked.

"Of course it helps, but there will not be a meeting tonight. Why can it not wait?" he continued to probe. "I am certain it would not make a difference whether or not we waited."

"True though that may be, Mistress Ehiztaria does prefer to know of things well in advance, and I cannot blame her, for it is rather embarrassing to not know whom you are addressing when you are leading a Clan such as ours!"

"Aye, aye. That would be bad. Of course we should speak with her."

"I thought you would see it my way." He chuckled. "Well, because there is not an actual meeting today, we shall have to meet with her at her own home. The trail is too difficult for a horse to maneuver, so we will have to take the path by foot. No matter, though. We have much time before anyone back at the castle will be expecting anything of us, no?"

He nodded, though he knew it was not true on his part. Princess Dawn would be waiting for him in the forest at dusk. It would break his heart were he not to be able to show up to their secret meeting. He had already missed out on so many due to surprise hunts in the forest to track down a pesky centaur or annoying unicorn. His list of excuses for being late was beginning to grow shorter and shorter each day.

"Alright, then! This way," Asher said, turning onto an over grown pathway that looked as though the last time a person had set foot upon it was never. "At her home, she does not go by Ehiztaria. She goes by Elizabeth," he continued to inform. "She lives alone, but she does not want any stray ears to hear her true identity, for her name is all over England by now. There are some on this Earth who seek to join us, some who ignore us, and others who seek to destroy us. That is why all meetings are held beneath the old hollow oak that is guarded by knock and password."

"Sounds rather logical," he said, bobbing his head up and down. "Technically speaking, if a person were to hate the Hunters and kill them for killing the magical creatures, are they not being hypocrites?"

"That is a touchy subject, Paul, for no one can really answer it, though I can tell you that they would have to be a complete idiot to go up against the Orion Clan! Though they may pick off one or two, eventually the Clan would step in and kill them as well," he explained. "Why? You were not thinking of rebelling were you?"

Sir Paul laughed. "Ah, Sir Asher! I see you still have a bit of wit left in you, old man!" He nudged his arm jokingly. "I was not asking you so much for my sake as your own!"

"Oh, really?" Asher asked. Before Paul could say another word, he jumped on top of him and pinned him to the ground. "Not such a jester now, are you?"

"I am not a jester, but a knight! And though you claim to be a knight, I find you more like a sunrise! So bright and cheery!" he jested, wrestling his uncle so that he was now on top.

He continued to chuckle. "Alright, alright, Paul! You got me! Now, if you would not mind letting me back on my feet..."

Paul jumped off and offered him his hand which he took with much thanks. "Are we there yet?" he asked.

"Almost. Just beyond that patch of sycamore trees." He continued walking, though he did not say another word to his nephew, for there was nothing left to say.

CHAPTER 20

Once the duo broke through the final band of sycamores, they came to a rather large clearing. In its center was a tiny thatch cottage with smoke billowing out of a crude stone chimney. It formed faux storm clouds above the otherwise peaceful looking home.

"This does not seem like a home for the leader of a hunting clan," Paul inquired.

"That is the point, Paul! Were you not paying attention the whole time I explained it to you back in the woods? Nonetheless, remember to address her solely as Elizabeth," Asher replied. "Are you ready?"

"It is not like she is going to stab me again," he said with a roll of his eyes.

"Whatever you say. Come now." He walked up to the door and did a series of loud and quiet knocks to alert Mistress Ehiztaria, or, rather, Elizabeth, of the forth coming Orion Clan members.

"The door is open! Please, do come in!" the woman called from within her home.

Asher pushed open the door and motioned for Paul to head inside before he himself followed suit.

"Greetings, Elizabeth," Paul said, nodding his head to her in acknowledgment.

"Ah, Paul... Is that you? I can scarcely tell with you clad all in silver!" Elizabeth laughed, getting up from her seat in front of the fireplace. "What brings you two to my humble abode?"

"Paul has some splendid news he wishes to share with you, Elizabeth," Asher replied.

"Oh, he does? Please, Paul! Do tell good old Elizabeth!" she chirped, watching him with growing interest. "I am to believe it has to do with your silver attire?"

"Today was my ceremony of knighthood. I am now officially Sir Paul Laurence Hunter of Asthla," he told her, pulling out his sword and holding it out so that she might see.

"Paul! This is wonderful news! I cannot believe it! It seems like only yesterday that you were but a wee page!" She pulled him into a hug. "I am very proud of you, boy! You stuck to it! This is wonderful!" She released him.

"Thank you kindly, Elizabeth. I am looking forward to better serving you and my kingdom," he told her, returning the sword to its scabbard on his hip. "I must say that this would not have happened without the assistance of you, the clan, and my uncle! To you, my life is indebted." He lowered his head.

She laughed. "Ah, such a bold, young spirit you have, child. If only I could have that kind of vigor!" She patted him on his armoured shoulder. "Keep that fire in your heart! It will keep your life burning on down wonderful roads!" After she spoke, she returned to her chair. "If you would not mind, I would like to speak solely to your uncle for a moment."

"Of course, Elizabeth," Paul said, leaving the house while his uncle went forward to speak with her. Normally, secret conversations only made him wish to continue listening in the cover of the shadows, but, for today, he settled with sitting outside the cottage and waiting for his uncle. His only desire right now was to hurry home so that he might meet with his love by the side of the brook, but it did not seem as though he would be on time. The sun was already almost to the horizon, and it would take them a few hours to return to the castle. With a heavy sigh, he waited.

"Yes, Elizabeth. Of course. I will see to it," Asher said as he backed out of the cottage and shut the door.

"What was that about, Uncle?" he asked.

"Matters that do not concern you. Can you find your own way back to the castle? I have some business to take care of on the other side of the forest," he replied, not even bothering to wait for Paul's answer before running off.

"Suuuuure, Uncle. Do not worry yourself with me! I am sure I can find my way back going through an unknown part of the forest I've only been through *once*. But, no matter..." he mumbled, kicking at the dirt as he sulked back into the forest. He could just *feel* the love from his uncle.

As he walked, he plucked a shadow from a nearby tree and began to twist it in his hands. "The nerve of that man... How could he just abandon his own nephew? He is no better than my dirty, rotten, no good, idiot father!" he hissed, throwing the shadow roughly to the ground. "I hope something terrible shall befall him on his journey..."

The sun was already at the horizon, and it was growing dark. He changed his course so that he would be heading for the brook rather than the castle. It would not make a difference whether he went to the castle first! No one would be there waiting for him. He figured it best just to go to the brook.

He quickly found the running water and followed it to the spot where he always met with Princess Dawn. She was not there yet herself, which seemed rather odd. He supposed that she had only been caught up with a suitor or perhaps was talking to her father and waiting for a chance to slip out. Keeping these thoughts in mind, he sat down by the water and began to undo some of the heavy and rather uncomfortable armour. For as glamorous as it looked, it was highly illogical.

Once he was clad in only the simple tunic and leggings he had worn beneath his suit of armour, he began to worry. There had still been no sign of Princess Dawn coming near. "I have been late so many times, it matters not," he mumbled to himself. He lay down on the grass. "Perhaps I can take a quick nap. She will wake me when she draws near..."

He curled up on the cool, soft grass at the brook's side and listened to it tell its unfathomable story time and time again. The long, arduous path he had walked upon to get there had left him well beyond tired, and it did not take long for the boy to drift into an extremely deep slumber.

CHAPTER 21

When Paul awoke, it was not because of Princess Dawn speaking to him, nor was she nudging his shoulder to figure out why it was that he was asleep and not waiting for her to come to him. It was, instead dawn's first light that pulled him from the world of dreams. He looked around and chewed on his lower lip. Where was she?

"Perhaps the King was watching her too closely. Maybe she just could not get out last night. I am sure all is well," he thought aloud, gathering up the pieces to his armour and heading back to the castle.

He sneaked past the guards on duty in the cover of the shadows, and he remained within them until he made it to the quarters he used to share with his uncle. Surely the King would allow him to move into another room. It seemed rather odd to sleep in the same room as his uncle when he no longer worked for him.

After placing the armour down upon his bed, he noticed that Sir Asher had not slept in his bed at all. The sheets were still ruffled the same way that he had seen them the other day upon passing his room. That was not much of a surprise, for whatever task Mistress Ehiztaria sent him on would more than likely have taken the entire night, and he himself would just be returning to Asthla that day.

Once he was dressed in fresh clothes with the Asthlan wyvern upon his breast and his daggers tucked into his secret pockets, he walked toward the throne room.

The knight guarding the door nodded to him in acknowledgment. "The King has been awaiting your presence, Sir Paul," he said, pushing the mighty oaken door open and allowing Paul to follow.

He fiddled with the collar of his shirt, feeling a bit of perspiration on the back of his neck. How could the King possibly be expecting him? "My Liege..." he said, kneeling before the King.

"Please, do arise, Sir Paul!" the King replied, his voice wavering.

Stiffly, he stood up. "You have been waiting for me, your Highness?"

"Indeed, Sir Paul. You spoke to my daughter after the knighthood ceremonies, did you not?" he asked, wringing his hands quickly.

"Aye, I did. She wished to congratulate me on making it to the rank of knight after having gone through training for the past ten years. Might I ask why this concerns you so?"

"Did she say anything about where she would be going at night?" he continued to question.

"No. I am afraid she did not make mentions of any plans. Where is she now?"

"No one knows! Oh, Sir Paul! Please tell me you would know!" he begged.

"I wish I could tell you now, but I cannot. However, give me but a day to search for the answer, and I shall bring to you information of her whereabouts," he said, trying to keep his own voice from shaking as much as the King's.

"The Princess's safety is of utmost importance. I shall not let you down, your Majesty!"

"Please. Go now and seek out the information that you can! Come back at sun down and tell me what you have discovered! I would give anything for my daughter's safe return!" he sobbed.

"But of course," he said, bowing his head before turning and leaving the throne room.

Once he was out of the King's sight, his hands balled into fists. Who would do such a thing to the Princess? He shook his head fiercely and ran out of the castle. He had to get to the bottom of this perplexing case, and he *would* get down to the bottom!

The first place he went to was the castle wall where he had spoken to Princess Dawn only a day ago. There were long shadows cast about it. With a growl, he pulled one from the ground and began to shake it violently. "Tell me where the Princess is, you worthless sliver of darkness!" he hissed, slamming it against the stone wall.

"I know not where the Princess is," it replied in a wispy hiss. "I am but the shadow of the castle. Nothing has gone on in my presence. The only thing I have witnessed was your meeting yesterday. Afterward, Princess Dawn said something about retiring to her quarters. That is all I know!" It oozed out from between his fingers and sunk back into place.

"Her room..." Paul mumbled. He took off in a sprint towards the room where the Princess had before mentioned that she would dwell in while she awaited him to return from the countless battles, training sessions, and meetings.

Never before had he actually entered into the Princess's room. It was nothing like he had imagined it, at least in the area of colour. Her four post canopy bed was draped with the finest green fabrics, and the plush rug on her floor resembled the colour of the grass that grew abundantly at the babbling brook's side. Other than that, her room was fairly plain and well organized, save for the fact that there was a single book thrown from her shelves.

Cautiously, Paul walked over and plucked the book off the floor. One page was folded, so he slowly flipped to it. A tiny note on coarse parchment fell out. In barely discernible letters, it read:

Dear Paul,

We had warned you five years ago! You did not heed our warning. Now your beloved Princess Dawn will die the most horrible death! We shall give you a hint, just to make you squirm even more: The creature that shall feast upon her is large and scaly and just loves to roast its meat before eating it! Good luck, Sir Paul! You are going to need it!

He blinked back tears as he read the note. His Princess was to be fed to a dragon! A dragon of all creatures! He shook his head. "I cannot let this happen!" Swiftly, he moved to the bed and picked up its shadow.

"Please, creation of the dark. Tell me who it is that has taken my Princess!" he begged, holding it tightly so that it could not leave. "Who is it, oh shadow? Who!?!"

"Their names I know not," the shadow said with a voice much like the castle's shadow, though it was closer to a human's voice than the latter had been, "but their faces I remember well! One bore a long scar that traversed from his cheek to his ear. His eyes were the color of ice and his hair the colour of snow. He adorned clothes of the purest red. He never once touched the Princess but instructed the others.

"Alongside him was a stout man. Everything about him was dark, from his hair to his eyes to his clothes. Even his skin was of a deep brown. He was the one who knocked the Princess unconscious from behind before binding and gagging her.

"The final man was large, both in height and size. His hair was a deep blonde, a mess upon the top of his head. His eyes were a piercing green that watched the Princess keenly. He hefted her upon his shoulders and carried her away with his other friends. Do with this information as you will, for I have told you all I know!" Like the first, this shadow slipped through the gaps in his fingers and disappeared back onto the floor.

Paul's legs buckled out from beneath him and he knelt on the ground, staring blankly at the floor. "Those men will pay dearly for what they have done... I shall rest at nothing to find them and bring them to justice!" He balled up his fists tightly and pounded them into his thighs. "I cannot let them turn my beloved into food for a hungry dragon..."

CHAPTER 22

As the day drew near to its closing, Paul returned to the King. "I bear both glad tidings and terrible news. Shall I tell you the good first?" he asked.

The King shook his head. "Start with the terrible. Please. Let me know what it is that is going on! I must have my daughter back! She is my only heir!" he begged.

"Very well, your Highness. Your daughter has been kidnapped by a group of men and taken off to be killed by a mighty creature in the near future," he said, biting his lip to keep from crying out at the news himself.

The King, however, was not so good at hiding his emotion. He collapsed on the arm rest of his throne and wailed. "My child! My dear, beloved child! Sent to her doom! Oh, why, cruel fate? Why would you take her! Please, dear Sir Paul! Please, tell me what it is that you call good news!"

"I have acquired the faces of the thieves who have kidnapped Princess Dawn," Paul said.

"That is hardly good news!" he cried out. "Faces mean nothing! There are thousands of faces in this world!"

110

"Please, your highness! I know that I can find these people whom have taken the Princess."

"Sir Paul... If you can find my daughter and bring her back alive, I shall owe you dearly! Just name the price at which you will find her! Money is not an object! I can pay you with many fabulous riches!"

"It is not wealth that I seek. If, or rather *when,* I bring back your daughter, my only wish is for her hand in marriage," Paul said, hoping that he was not being too bold.

"Then that shall be your reward!" he replied, too distraught to question his motives. "Bring back my daughter, and I shall make her yours forever! Just bring her back alive! I am begging you, Sir Paul!"

"Of course, your Majesty. I shall return quickly, as if upon the wings of an eagle. The men who have done us wrong will be brought to justice! They shall pay for what they have done with their lives!" he said, scowling at the mere thought of the terrible men who had invaded the castle.

"Ah, Sir Paul! Such a young knight, yet such a bold, brave young man! I wish I could do more to assist you myself, but, alas, I cannot. I am not as young as I once was, and the King's place is in his castle among his people. Hurry back and I shall reward you generously!" he repeated.

"Nothing can stop me, your Majesty," he said and turned to leave. "If I am not back within the month, expect the worst, but do not expect the worst until the month has come to pass. I do not plan to fail!" With that he left.

He could hear the King mumble, "No one plans to, but still many do..."

Paul laughed to himself. "He should not hold me with such low esteem. Soon, he will learn not to underestimate the abilities of Sir Paul Laurence Hunter. Before his departure, he decided to pay one last visit.

"Hello, Father!" he spit in the face of the man whom he and his uncle had been keeping barely alive. "Do you remember me? I am certain you do! NOW!" He laughed cruelly.

Sir Laurence had learned it to be better if he did not say a word when his son came down to rant and then mock him some more.

"I thought you would be interested to know that I shall be leaving on a quest today. I will be slaying my first dragon. What do you think of that? Another magical creature, dying to the hands of *your own son*." Once more, he chuckled. "I shall see you upon my return."

He shook his head. "What have you come to, my son? Why would you be doing this...?"

"If you *must* know, I am going to save the Princess. Is that not a valiant thing for me to do?" he asked, puffing out his chest. "Farewell, father! I shall not see you for a long *long* time!" He turned on his heels and walked away.

"I thought I had raised you better," Sir Laurence mumbled as he left.

"Shut your mouth, old man!" he called over his shoulder along with a few choice words. He informed one of the guards to keep an eye on their special prisoner. Laurence was still his father and he still wanted him alive, even if his only motive was to torture him.

Once out of the dungeon, he gathered his belongings and a few rations before saddling up Umbra and riding out in search of the Princess. "I'll bring you home, Princess Dawn. Or I shall die at your side..."

CHAPTER 23

The first day's trip was a short one. He knew that he could not possibly find Princess Dawn on his first day, but he could only hope. Deciding it to be best to travel in only one direction, he headed for the direction of the setting sun. After leaving, it began to sink in how foolish that it was to begin such an epic journey at such a late hour. Nonetheless, every precious moment of every day counted. He kept his fingers crossed.

The first town he came to was rather quaint in appearance. There was but a single inn that he could find. Once inside, he could already hear the boisterous laughter of some men who had already had one beer too many. He rolled his eyes and sat down in front of the large table where a naïve girl was serving drinks.

"Why the long face, Sir Horse?" she chirped, smiling obliviously.

He managed a tiny smile. "I am in search of love," he sighed.

"Oh, love!" she crooned, lying down on the table, looking up at him. "Is it not... well... should we say... lovely?" She batted her eye lashes at him.

"I am not searching for *a* love. I am searching for *my* love," he clarified.

She pouted. "Oh. I see." In one fluid motion, she got up from the table. "Well, can I ask you what you wish to have?"

"Just some ale, please," he said, resting his chin upon his fists.

"Very well," she sighed, flicking her hair over her shoulder. She winked at a man at the table next to him as she went to go get Paul's order.

The man tottered over to him and sat down, raising his own mug. "Ah, boyee. Yer lookin' feh luuuuv?" he asked, smiling foolishly. "Why ya butherin' wit dat, anywayz? Whah doz ih mather?"

"I must find my fiancee. Her life is on the line, and I must save her!" Paul cried out.

He laughed, a little too boisterously. "Fiancée? Aye, laddy. Thas a gewd ohn! Ah gurl who ye cah luuuuv!" he said, waving his tanker around in the air.

The servant girl returned and handed him his beer. "Enjoy," she said to him. She looked at the other man and nodded.

"Ifth ye'll excuth meh," he said, getting up and walking out with the girl.

Paul rolled his eyes. "The load of imbeciles..." he mumbled with a shake of his head. He looked down at the beer that the servant girl had brought him. Though he had ordered it, he found no desire to drink it. His appetite was gone. All he could think about was his dear Princess Dawn, probably being fed to the dragon...

He shook his head. "Not yet," he told himself. Rising from his chair, he walked over to a man working behind the counter. "Might I bother you for a room?" he asked.

"Depends. Can you afford a room, Sir?" he replied.

In response, he held out a handful of gold coins. "Does that answer your question?"

He nodded. "Aye, Sir. Twenty pieces a night."

"Twenty pieces? You had better hope that room is worth it, else things shall end very VERY badly for a certain innkeeper and his maid servant," Paul told him, glaring at him with a stone cold gaze.

"Did I say twenty? I meant ten! My mind must be fumbling! Terribly sorry!" he blubbered.

"That sounds *much* more logical!" he laughed, passing off ten coins and taking the key from the innkeeper. "And now you must tell me something. Have you seen a band of men come by? One pale, one dark, and one in between?"

The man glanced around before moving in closer to Paul. "Indeed, Sir, I have! They came by the other day. They called themselves the 'Dawn Treaders.' Sounds like a rather odd name if you ask me." He shrugged.

"You must tell me where it was that they were headed!" Paul hissed, banging a fist on the table. Of course they would call themselves the Dawn Treaders! They had taken his Dawn in the night.

"They merely said to the mountains. If you would not mind, you are causing a bit of an upset among the other visitors," he said, holding up his hands.

He growled. "Fine." He turned quickly and went up the stairs to his room. Out of the corner of his eyes, he could see the man and servant maid from before kissing in a dark hall. He hissed under his breath and clutched his fist. The shadows around the two constricted for a moment, knocking the two together roughly and then separating them.

"JERK!" the maid servant hissed, slapping the drunkard across the face as she rubbed her aching head.

"Whah dih Ah dew?" he asked.

Paul laughed to himself. "Idiots..." Then, he headed up the stairs to his room.

As he sat upon his bed, he shook his head. It was a bit of serendipity to find out the whereabouts of the three thieves who had taken his wife to be. Only one problem came to mind: the mountains were a vast area. It could take forever to actually find the right part of the mountains. No matter, he would certainly find it. Nothing could keep him away from this goal of his. Once his mind was set upon something, it was set there permanently and would refuse to detach itself until he had accomplished it.

He laid down then and stared up at the ceiling. If only he could find Princess Dawn that very night. All would have been well at that point. Unfortunately, that was not true, and he knew it would not be true for a long time. He sighed deeply and closed his eyes. What could he do? He was simply one person, and he was human enough to need rest and nutrition. That was the fact that hurt him the most. When he was a pure spirit, these things were not even a thought to him. Now that he had a human host, however, they were necessary.

With a shake of his head, he turned his gaze to the window. Why did he even care so much about her? He knew that his love was growing, but he had not realized the true extent of his feelings until now. It felt as though the woman had truly taken a piece of his heart with her when she was taken away from him. One hand absentmindedly covered his heart. "Oh, Princess Dawn..." he whispered. "I cannot wait to see you again, but I shall see you again! I promise!"

He curled up into a ball on the covers and decided to let the conscience have a moment. Of course, the conscience began to cry and moan. "I cannot lose Princess Dawn! I have already lost my mother! I do not need to lose another!" he whimpered. He rubbed the tears from his eyes with the back of his hands and felt as though someone was wrapping their arms around him.

"All shall be fine, my little Paulie. I have been watching over you, and I will continue to watch over you until it is your time to join me on the other side," a woman whispered behind him.

He turned around to see his mother lying down beside him. "Thank you," he whispered. He tried to kiss her cheek, but she pulled away from him and disappeared before he could make contact with her.

The spirit thought it better to take over at that point. "Idiot child," he thought aloud. "What were you thinking? Trying to meet with your mother? Why would you even think of doing that?" He laughed and uncurled. "You are such a stupid person." With a final laugh, he closed his eyes and went to rest for the night.

CHAPTER 24

As soon as the sun was up once more, Paul was out of bed. He threw the key down on the counter in front of the half awake innkeeper before he ran out and mounted Umbra once more. "Quickly, Umbra," he whispered, snapping the reigns against the horse's black neck. "We have no time to waste! Go, Umbra!"

The horse whinnied loudly before running off in the direction he was steered in.

Many people watched in amazement as they saw the man clad in shining armour with a wyvern upon his breast plate. Never before had they seen a knight come through this part of the village. Many children walked forth to meet him, but Paul paid them no mind as he raced on.

"I have heard he is on a quest," one gossip said to another. "He is in search of King Arthur's holy grail!"

"Nonsense," the other replied. "I have heard that he has gone off in search of King Midas's treasure!"

"Alas, both of you are wrong!" the man from the night before said, rubbing his aching temples from the severe hangover he was recovering from. "He is in search of a fair maiden, one to whom he is betrothed!"

The women gasped. "Such a valiant deed for a knight to perform! Why could he not be in search of a peasant girl?" the first swooned.

Paul just shook his head to this conversation. "My heart beats solely for Princess Dawn! I shall find her and bring her home, lest I die!" he called over to them.

"Such dedication! Why can my husband not be more like him?" the second woman sighed deeply as she walked off to go find the man of whom she had spoken of.

Without another word, Paul rode on. He could not spend any more time wasted on idle chit chat with the locals. He needed to find Princess Dawn soon and speaking only cost him more and more time.

Once he left the village, he found himself in an old graveyard. Umbra was forced to go no faster than a trot as he danced over and around the headstones. It was an exceedingly difficult task, so Paul got off of the mount. The shade within him could not help but wish to examine this land further. One point of interest was a freshly dug hole, still open without a body inside. Stranger yet was the fact that there was another hole beside it.

Carefully, he read the inscriptions upon the stones. The words he read gripped his heart with an icy fear. One read the name, "Dawn Ella Rayland" and the other read "Paul Laurence Hunter." This sent a sudden shiver down his spine. Why were these graves even here?

With much anger and abhorrence, he ripped the stones from the ground and hurled them into the holes, kicking the dirt back into its rightful place. "How dare they! The nerve of them! They would have been better off to dig up their own grave than to dig ours!"

He grabbed the reigns of Umbra and tugged her away, out of the cemetery. "Oh, they shall pay dearly with their lives! Never should one have gotten so cocky with Sir Paul!"

Once they were clear of the last headstone, he mounted again and rode off, pushing Umbra to his limits and then some.

A forest went by beside them in a blur, only allowing Paul to see glimpses of what was within it. There was a bird here, a squirrel there. Had he not been in so much of a rush, he would have stopped for a quick hunt for he had seen tiny blips of things that would have led him straight to a prized unicorn, but he could not afford another moment to waste. Instead, he continued on his journey.

When the sun was high in the sky, he took a break for a moment to water his horse and fill his own stomach with some salted meats he had brought along. He glanced at the forest once more and nibbled his lip. Though it would cost him time to search for the unicorn, the horn would prove to be a valuable tool on his journey.

"Umbra, wait out here. Should someone come by, run for cover in the forest," he instructed.

The horse bobbed its head up and down, as though it understood his English with perfect fluency. With a stamp of its hoof, it stood its ground and waited for Paul.

The boy stripped himself of his armour, leaving only the tunic and leggings on to allow for easier maneuvering and to prevent the creature from hearing him approach. He clutched his daggers tightly and glanced around. There was a rub mark upon one of the trees, smooth in comparison to those made by bucks. He smirked and followed it to yet another rub mark.

On the ground, there was a faint trail of hoof prints left by the easily distinguished cloven hooves of the unicorn. He remained within the shadows, disappearing from sight as he followed the tracks. Snagged on a nearby tree branch was a lock of black hair, likely from a mane. Things were starting to look up for him. The hoof prints were growing more distinct as he went further and further into the woods until he came upon a place that he could not truly consider a field but merely a tiny break in the forest.

In the center of the place lay a unicorn, though it appeared to already have been killed by something else. He frowned in utter disappointment. How could he have followed such a false trail? There was a pool of crimson blood with a slight metallic shine to it, the sign that it was indeed shed from a unicorn and no other beast.

Paul sighed as he approached the creature. He observed three claw marks that raked down its side and flank. How terrible... Not really. It appeared as though a bear had come after the creature, for the horn was still intact. No creature would ever bother to eat the horn, though humans, such as Paul, enjoyed stealing them for their own use. With a skillful slice, he removed the horn and tucked it into his pocket when he heard a rustle in the bushes behind him.

He turned around quickly and was met by a large beast that looked extremely feline. It was odd for those parts, for no cats were known to dwell in the area. He raised an eyebrow and pulled out his daggers.

"Foolish human... Falling for the bait!" the creature cackled in a feminine voice. Its body began to shake as the fur melted away to flesh and the bones shifted to a more humanoid shape. Though the tail and ears remained, the creature stood upright. "Looks like my dinner has arrived!"

"I fear you are mistaken, miss, for I am no one's meal," Paul replied, holding his daggers at the ready once more.

"What are you going to do? Stab me to death? I am so frightened! No one shall ever pass I, the Guardian of the Forest, Arisbane!" she continued to taunt. "Hold up your weapons, puny man. Show me how much of a fight you can put up!" She held up her hands, claws bent for the easiest and most efficient method of striking.

A smile played upon his lips. "Oh, you shall be surprised what I can do." He laughed stiffly, twirling the daggers so that he could hold them in the manner of an assassin, the most agile method he had yet to learn from the Orion Clan. "Make my day!"

Arisbane made the first move, rushing at him with unbelievable speed. When he attempted to dodge, her claws dug into his shoulder, raking through the fabric and flesh. She laughed evilly and licked the blood from her claws. "Delicious..." she mumbled, her eyes rolling up in joy.

He took that moment to be his moment to strike. In a quick, fluid motion, he shot his dagger out and forced it into her side.

The cat woman yowled in pain and pawed at her wound. "You shall pay for what you have done to me!" she hissed, running at him again. Half way there, she morphed once more into her full cat form and pounced on him.

There was an "oof" as he was thrown to the ground, her claws biting into his flesh. He growled fiercely. "You have until the count of three to get off of me!"

"You do not frighten me. Besides, I am over top you. You pose no threat to me!" she laughed, continuing to inflict pain upon him.

"One... Two... Three!" Once he said three, he flicked his hand at her side. A shadow rose up from the ground and entwined itself around her waist, pulling her from him.

She hissed angrily and refused to release her grip, though the shadow tugging on her eventually forced her. With a pout, she continued to attempt to swipe at him. "You are a wimp! Fight like a man!" she complained. "You are a coward! Do not behave as such!"

"It would be unfair of you to be allowed to use your advantages of being half demon if I were not allowed to use my own powers!" he protested, throwing her down to the ground.

"True, true..." she said, tail twitching in frustration. She shook quickly before jumping onto her paws. With another fluid motion, she was upon him once more.

It took only a wave of Paul's cloak to disappear from her sight and ruin her chances of finding him. He laughed to himself. "Silly kitten!" he mocked.

"Where did you go?" she shouted out with much aggravation. "Why are you still being a coward? Show your face!" Frantically, she ran back and forth through the forest.

Meanwhile, Paul had made it well away from her and was already leaving the forest with his prize: the unicorn's horn. He left the shield of the shadows and whistled loudly. Faithfully, Umbra ran to his side and bowed his head to him.

He chuckled. "Good boy, Umbra," he whispered, patting his mane. "Come. Quickly. We must leave before Arisbane can find us!" With great speed, he got atop the horse and spurred him. As they left, he could hear Arisbane. It was obvious that that would not be his only encounter with the demented forest guardian.

CHAPTER 25

There were fewer and fewer towns the closer he got to the mountains over the next few days. Apparently, many people feared whatever creature was guarding the mountains at the time. He shook his head as thoughts of exactly what it was that would be guarding the mountains he sought. A shiver ran down his spine, gripping him with fear for the future.

Umbra stopped at the corner of the forest, head lowered with fatigue. He turned his head, a large eye pleading with Paul to let him rest.

"Very well. We shall set up camp here," he said, digging a hole in the ground and pouring the horse some water.

Gratefully, the horse drank. Being so weary, he contented himself with lying down and nibbling on some brush beside his head.

Paul walked over to him and removed the saddle and reigns from Umbra to make things a bit more comfortable before he himself sat down in the grass, nibbling upon a piece of bread from the previous night's stay at the inn.

True, it was stale, but it was better than starving. He shuddered once more as he thought of his poor fiancée, doubting that she got any nourishment herself.

Princess Dawn... The image of her was horrific. The light that usually graced her body had faded in his thoughts, leaving her dull and dark. Her once luscious curls were now limp, clinging to her head tightly. His image of her body appeared far thinner and much less healthy. It was her eyes that made him cringe. In his mind, he saw her eyes as being the dullest feature of her entire being, absorbing all light and refusing to release any of it back to the Earth.

He shunned these thoughts from himself. There was no desire within him to think of her as he would find her, but only to see her as she was and would be once he rescued her. When they were in the castle together, she always had an iridescent glow about her. Her eyes twinkled like the stars. Everything about her was just perfect.

A sigh escaped his lips as he continued his thoughts, no longer looking at her as he last remembered. He decided to look at her as how she would grow to be once they were together again and happily wedded. The shine in her eyes that had once been mere stars would grow to be blazing suns showing the true joy of her inner soul and his own as well. This brought yet another smile to his mouth. They would no longer only confess their love to the brook and the surrounding trees. It would become known to the world, and together, their reign would spread over all regions, proclaiming their conquering love that could survive anything that was thrown at them.

Indeed, it would be with this love that he would finally reign victorious unlike the various other times he had tried taking over the world within the bodies of Genghis Khan or Alexander the Great. Love was the missing component in all of these attempts, and he had finally solved that most complex riddle. Princess Dawn would be his ticket to world domination, as well as to his own happiness, though he did not know if a spirit as dark as his could ever enjoy such a light feeling.

He lay down on the ground and stared up at the sky. "Oh, Princess Dawn..." he whispered to the twinkling stars above. "I will save you. Perhaps you shall even save me!"

A rustle in the bushes caused him to start, hand on his dagger. That blasted cat from before was back, and it was eying him carefully. "So... You seek Princess Dawn?" she asked with a purr.

"What do you want now?" he hissed. "Leave me be, and I shall not be wearing your pelt tomorrow!"

She laughed and returned to her somewhat human form. "Very well. Perhaps I should leave. I merely thought you would care to know more about this Dawn whom you are seeking. Then again, I must have been mistaken." Slowly, she turned around and began to walk off.

"Wait... Why would you help me? You just tried to kill me, banshee cat!" he shouted after her.

With a slight pause, she turned to look at him. "The men whom took your *precious* Princess Dawn are the very ones who killed the former Guardian of the Forest, as well as the Guardian of the Mountain, forcing great imbalances in power among our creatures as they fought for the title."

"If this is a trick, it is rather poorly fabricated," he said with a roll of his eyes.

"I kid you not, boy! They truly have killed many, just as they plan to kill Princess Dawn! They are going to feed her to the new Guardian of the Mountains! They shall be there in two days!" she went on. "I knew not that you were after these men! Had I known, I would not have attacked you. I feared that you were working for them and attacked because I fretted you would bring harm to my forest!"

He continued to sit on the ground, shaking his head. "Preposterous... You are telling lies to me!"

"Sir, you must believe me! One was dark as the forest floor, the other white as a cloud while yet another was large with hair the colour of the sand! The Dawn Treaders!" she shouted.

That finally caught his attention. "The Dawn Treaders?" he asked.

"Indeed, Sir! I will help you retrieve your love if you would only help me to kill these three men! Please, Sir!" she begged.

"I shall help you, Arisbane, so long as you grant me protection in your forest."

"You will have to earn it, but, for now, you shall be protected. After we encounter the Dawn Treaders, then shall I decide the rest of your fate within my woods," she said, clicking her claws against a tree's bark.

"You have a deal," he said, shaking hands with the cat woman. "For now..." he added. He thought he had said it aloud, but it was merely a thought inside his idle mind. "In the morning we shall travel, for my steed is still too weary."

"The horse will slow us down. Leave it here," she instructed.

Paul glared at her with a steely look. "I will *not* leave my horse!"

"The animals of the forest shall treat him well. We need to keep moving. The Dawn Treaders scarcely rest, and that horse will need far too much rest each night," she pointed out.

After a quick glance at his beloved horse, he sighed. "Very well. But if anything should happen to Umbra, it will be your blood that shall pay the atonement for it!" he hissed.

She held up her hands innocently. "I promise I shall let little harm come to your horse."

"Change that little to a no, or else the horse stays in our party."

"Very well. *No* harm shall come to your horse. Now we must go! Hurry!" she said, already trying to pull him up off his feet.

"I can walk, thank you very much," he complained, getting up. He turned once more to Umbra. "I shall return to you soon." He kissed the horse between the ears.

Umbra nodded his head lazily and nudged his arm in farewell. Then, he laid his head down once more and drifted off to sleep.

Paul grabbed some of the saddle bags and tied them to some loops concealed within his cloak. "I am ready, Arisbane," he said.

She nodded curtly and began to run, shifting back into a large cat in the process.

With a sigh, he followed after her. Though he still did not trust this strange cat girl who claimed to be the Guardian of the Forest, she would prove to be an asset to him. Overall, the day had been fairly productive. Not only did he know who Princess Dawn's captors were, he also knew to where they planned to bring her and to whom she would be sacrificed. True, it was not all good news to hear, but it was still good news to aid in his search for these men.

As he ran, he continued to watch Arisbane. There had to be some kind of ulterior reason for her to do what it was that she was doing. Certainly one does not try to kill someone one moment and then befriend them the next in sheer chivalry. After all, he was a master of deception, and this certainly seemed like a plan to deceive. Still, he could not simply put her down as a total foe. She had been of some assistance as of that moment, so he told himself that she must not be all bad if she was trying to help him. All that he could hope was that she would remain true to her word and lead him to his beloved Princess. Princess Dawn was the only thing that mattered to him now, strange as it seemed. Not even his own life mattered to him. The only thing he continued to envision was himself standing before the priest, ready to be married.

CHAPTER 26

Barely able to catch their breaths, the unlikely duo stopped at the base of the mountains. Arisbane looked up with a frown. "It's a long way up..." she mumbled, shaking her head. "Do you climb well? I sure hope you can do so quickly..." Her eyes were focused on something far overhead.

"What do you mean, Arisbane? Of course, I can climb very fast. What are you watching?" Sir Paul tried to follow the gaze of the cat woman, but he failed in doing so.

"They have already arrived here. We will have to travel even faster if we wish to catch up to them," she said, climbing despite the fact that she was breathing heavily as it was.

"How could they possibly have beaten us here?" he asked, trying to keep up with her. Both were slowed considerably.

"It is no use..." Arisbane moaned after getting only a few yards away from the ground. "We shall never be able to catch up with them tonight. Rest for now. We cannot risk our lives for the sake of retrieving this one girl. It is highly unlikely that they will sacrifice her tonight, besides. The Dawn Treaders seem to be slowing down. In the morning, we shall catch up. Worry not!"

With a sigh, he paused to rest on the mountain's ledge. "Very well, but I shall be holding you accountable for her life," he told Arisbane, crossing his arms on his lap and resting his chin upon them.

"I assure you, all will be well," she repeated, curling up into a ball by his side. Her eyes slowly closed.

Paul shook his head as he watched her. She had been in such a rush, and now all she wanted to do was take a cat nap. Princess Dawn was within their sight, and she was resting! His hands curled up into fists as he glared at the sleeping girl. Why would she do that to him? It was so important for him to get Princess Dawn back, yet she did not seem to care. This was putting their alliance into question.

While the cat woman slept, she pawed playfully at the air, shaking her head and moving her tail back and forth. A tiny roar escaped her as she chased after whatever it was that she was chasing in her dreams. She seemed very intent on catching up to whatever creature she was chasing.

Why was she so focused on this creature in her dreams when she could not even focus on getting Princess Dawn, whom was real and in actual danger? He shook his head. Asking her for help, or rather, agreeing to let her help was a big mistake on his part. All he could hope for was that Princess Dawn would not be killed while they sat on the side of the mountain.

With all of this on his mind, he looked up the rocky crags of the mountain. Now, he could make out the group of men. Sure enough, they were the same ones that the shadow had told him about. The bulky blonde was still holding onto someone whom he could only assume to be Princess Dawn, though he was not sure. It was apparent that the person the man was holding was feminine, but it looked nothing like the regal woman that had been at the castle only days before.

The woman that he was carrying had hair caked to her head with dirt and mud. That was highly unlike the Princess, for she was always kept clean and smelled of soap every day. He shook his head. There was no doubt in his mind that it was Princess Dawn, even though the woman did not look like her. She still held herself in the same way she always had.

Paul laid down by the side of Arisbane, continuing to watch the people as they, too, began to rest. He sighed with relief. At least they would not be getting much further during the night. He slowly closed his eyes and envisioned saving her.

CHAPTER 27

"Come on, man! Wake up! They are on the move! Get up! Stop sleeping!" a voice shouted at him while he rested. It was not until he could feel someone kicking his side that he realized what was going on. "GET UP!"

"I am up, I am up!" he moaned, pushing aside whatever was attacking him. He slowly rolled to a standing position and blinked at the bright sun's light. "Princess Dawn?" he asked.

The woman slapped him across the face, and he was knocked to his senses. "I am not Princess Dawn, idiot! Now, let us get going!" Arisbane hissed at him as she glared.

"Of course, of course..." he sighed, shaking his head. By the time he looked again, Arisbane was well over his head. He began to climb after her.

There was a great amount of distance between them and the Dawn Treaders. It was highly unlikely that they would catch up to them before they paused for another break, which would more than likely not be anytime soon. Adrenaline was pulsing throughout Sir Paul's entire body.

He could tell that he was getting close to once more being united with his fiancée.

His heart beat loudly in his chest. He wanted nothing less than being with Princess Dawn in safety. As he continued to climb, he became increasingly excited.

"Paul! Pay attention!" Arisbane shouted, catching him as he began to fall down.

He blinked and looked up. "Huh? What?" he stammered, glancing around. It had caught him unawares. Too much was on his mind and he had slipped. There were tiny scrapes on the tips of his fingers where he had lost his grip.

"Do not let that happen again! We cannot afford to fall down and have to climb all over again!" she chastised him. Her claws clicked as she ascended the mountain's side once more.

Paul followed her and watched the placement of his hands, not wishing to have another mishap.

And so their ascent went on without further interruption. They had reached the precipice of the mountain and could now walk a bit more due to its flat top. He could already see Princess Dawn chained to the rock, just as he had expected to see her. She was looking down at the ground in front of her, tears welling up in her eyes. The Dawn Treaders were nowhere to be seen.

"Princess Dawn!" Sir Paul called out.

The woman gasped and looked around quickly until her eyes stopped, locked on his. "Oh, Sir Paul!" she cried out, trying to run to him. The chains restrained her, forcing her to cease her struggling. "Oh, Sir Paul! Please, do come hither!"

He ran, ignoring Arisbane's constant shouting as he did so. "Is it truly you, Princess Dawn?" he asked.

Princess Dawn nodded. "Of course, my knight! Please! Help me! They told me that I would become a sacrifice! A sacrifice, Sir Paul! I cannot die!" she cried.

Tears streaked down her filthy cheeks, leaving wet trails in their path.

"Stop struggling, Princess Dawn. Do not speak! I shall help you!" he said, tugging on the chains. They refused to give way.

"PAUL! Stop! The Dawn Treaders are returning!" Arisbane called out.

Paul glanced up and saw the threesome approaching them. His jaw was set in a harsh scowl as he watched them. "Those are the men who have taken you?" he asked, his lips scarcely even moving.

The Princess nodded ever so slowly. "The dark one, their leader, his name is Nigel. That white one, he goes by Ethan. That large one is called Duane," she replied, her eyes as wide as could be. "Beware of them, my knight of the night! Please, be careful!"

"I have fought scarier men than that in my travels. These men are not something that neither you nor I need to worry about!" he assured her. He ran off to meet them.

"Aw, look. A mere boy has been sent to stop us! How terribly frightening! Quick, men! We must run for our lives!" Nigel said, holding his hands up in mock surrender.

Duane laughed, loud and deep. "Alas! We shall not be threatened by such a weak opponent. I could just as easily crush his head between my hands as run from him."

"You underestimate me. I can defeat you, Duane, and I will never have to lay a finger on you!" Paul called back.

That got another chuckle out of Duane. "You are so full of yourself. You cannot do anything!"

Princess Dawn tried to kick at Sir Paul, but she could not reach him. "Sir Paul! What are you saying!?! You cannot take on Duane!" she shouted.

Paul just rolled his eyes and nodded. "Uh-huh... Uh-huh..." He moved a hand at his side and made a fist. The shadow at Duane's feet contracted around his legs like a boa constrictor. The overly large man was brought to the ground. "Told you!"

"How did you do that?" nearly everyone asked.

Nigel shook his head. "What do you think you are doing?" he asked. "Those simple little spells will do nothing for you!"

"Ah, but it was not a spell, good sir!" he replied.

With a scowl, Nigel began to run at Paul. That caused him to roll his eyes and clutch his fist once more. Nigel went down with a "thud" as his shadow wrapped around his legs from his ankles to his waist.

"Welcome to my chasse!" Paul called out to him. "I am the Hunter, you are my hunted!" He slipped the daggers out of his pockets and held them at the ready as the final member of the Dawn Treaders, Ethan, ran at him with a sword drawn.

It was obvious that Ethan was trained specifically in the art of brute force, for his moves were too definite and predictable. Paul easily sidestepped out of the way of the man's blade and caught it between his own two daggers, pulling it from his hands and tossing it aside like a twig. Before he could make another move, Arisbane ran over and jumped on the man's back.

"I'll teach you to mess with the Guardians of Nature!" she roared, clawing at his back.

Ethan screamed out in pain, but his companions were unable to help him for Paul had already begun to strangle them with their shadows. Within moments, the three captors lay on the mountain's floor, lifeless and motionless.

"That really wasn't much fun..." Paul complained, kicking the lifeless form of Nigel.

"Oh, Sir Paul! My knight! My hero!" Princess Dawn crooned, once more trying to break free from the chains that held her. All struggling ceased as a large, ominous shadow passed over the three living souls, and a dark quiet hung over them.

CHAPTER 28

The creature that owned the shadow hovered just above the chained Princess, watching its prey with its stone-cold black eyes. It never lifted them from the easy to obtain woman chained to the rock. It licked its lips hungrily.

Arisbane ran over. "Don't even think about it, lizard!" she hissed at the black dragon.

With a roll of its eyes, the dragon blew out a jet of flames that hit Arisbane. She shrieked in pain and shrunk back.

"Arisbane!" Paul shouted, but he could not worry about her. There was no time. The dragon was already lowering its mighty jaws. "Unhand my Princess, foul beast!"

"Never, mortal! She shall be my feast!" the dragon replied, turning its gaze upon him.

"I will never leave this mountain without her by my side!"

"And many with your vigor have often died."

"Unhand my Princess, I say!"

"You shall meet your maker today!" The dragon roared angrily and breathed out another plume of fire, aiming it carefully at his chest.

"PAUL!!!" Princess Dawn screeched, straining against the chains with even more force.

Sir Paul ignored her as he lifted up his cloak, disappearing into the shadows. This caused the dragon to growl in frustration. He merely laughed, knowing he now had the upper hand. Without a word, he sneaked around the shadows, heading for the dragon.

The dragon turned its large head quickly from side to side. Seeing that his mobile prey was nowhere in sight, he once more bent over to ingest the sacrifice left for him. He froze midway to her as something plunged into his stomach.

While in the shadows, Paul had recovered Ethan's sword and was now shoving it through the soft flesh of the dragon's stomach, pushing it with all of his strength. The dragon roared and groaned in pain, swatting its large talons at its attacker. Due to his massive size, he could not see and continually missed the mark.

His attacker, however, was small in size and was also quite agile. Time after time he plunged the sword into the soft flesh, watching as the blood flowed out from the various wounds. The blade of Ethan's sword was stained red. He grinned and ducked out from beneath the beast.

The dragon roared, trying to breathe more fire at Paul, though only a few sparks were emitted from its mouth. The strength had left its body. It roared again, though very mournfully. There was no way for the Guardian of the Mountain to fight back. As it collapsed on the ground, a smaller black dragon ventured over to see what was going on.

Paul moved to attack the new dragon, but it flew off while crying out something about his father. It was out of sight within moments. After a brief pause, Paul moved his focus back to Princess Dawn. He cut the chains with a fierce blow from Ethan's sword. As soon as her arms were free, she threw them around his neck.

"You truly are my hero!" she crooned, holding onto him tightly. "Oh, I thought that I would never see you again!" She kissed his cheeks repetitively.

"Here. Drink this," he said, cupping some of the dragon's fresh blood. He held it up to her.

She stared at it. "What is that?" she asked, her knees shaking.

"Just trust me on this one, Princess Dawn. You know that I would never bring harm to you. Drink it!" he said, pushing it at her once more.

With a worried sigh, she held out her hands, and Paul poured it into them. She drank it and felt a bit better, more stable.

"Now was that so terribly bad?" Paul asked.

"Are you going to tell me what that was?"

He shook his head. "You do not want to know what it was." After handing a rag to Princess Dawn so that she might clean her hands, he walked over to Arisbane, more blood cupped in his hands.

Arisbane lay on the side of the mountain's top. She had still scarcely moved since she was singed by the Guardian of the Mountain's plume of flame. Her hands were clutched over her chest which was badly burned.

With a cringe, Paul poured some blood onto the wound and then poured some more of the red liquid into Arisbane's mouth. He watched her carefully for any sign of change.

She sputtered for a moment, coughing up some of the blood. Her eyes slowly fluttered open. "Paul...?" she mumbled, blinking her eyes.

"Good. You are alive," he said, already leaving her side.

"Hey! Where are you going!?! You can't just leave me here!" she called after him. She tried to leap to her feet, but only succeeded in sending a wave of pain throughout her entire body. She cringed and fell back down.

Paul turned around and raised an eyebrow. "I never said I was going to leave you," he told her, grabbing the rag from Princess Dawn and wiping off his own hands. "We do have to get moving, however." He wrapped an arm around his wife to be. "Now. Get up slowly. You are still extremely injured."

Arisbane hissed and got to her feet. "I hate this human body..." she mumbled, trying to transform. Patches of fur appeared in varying places on her body, but she did not complete the transformation. With a sigh, she gave up and walked over to Paul. "How far do you plan on traveling?"

"Not far. You both are very weak, but we must get as far down the mountain as we can." He began to head over to the mountain's edge and looked down. "We need a rope..." Without another word, he went over to the dead bodies of the Dawn Treaders and began to search them for rope. He succeeded in finding a few lengths of rope. "Perfect."

He took the ropes over to the two girls and tied one length around each of their waists. "I shall lower you both one at a time. Try and climb as much as you can, but do not strain yourselves."

The duo nodded and began their descent down the mountain.

CHAPTER 29

Once at the mountain's base, it was already very dark. Paul shook his head. "We are not going to be able to travel for a while," he sighed, observing the worn women. "For tonight, we shall just head over to that village yonder. Tomorrow, we will rest and gather the necessary supplies. Does that sound like a good plan?"

Lazily, the two nodded. "We will need all the rest we can get," Princess Dawn chimed in.

"Agreed," the Guardian of the Forest added. Her feline ears flattened against her human head. "I do not feel well..." She tottered over a bit.

Instinctively, Paul reached out and caught her before she could hit the ground. "Come on, you two. You have certainly been out for far too long." He wrapped his arms around the shoulders of each of the women to support them lest they should totter and fall once more.

The village streets were filled with many people. They were full of energy, despite the late hour. "What is going on?" Paul asked a nearby man.

"It is the Festival of Orion! We celebrate the day that the Orion Clan was banished from our fair city! Even our King shall make an appearance. There have been reports of clan members within our city, and he hopes to seek them out and bring them to justice," the man explained.

"I see..." he mumbled. He unconsciously removed his hand from Princess Dawn's shoulder, the one that bore the mark of the Orion Clan. "Why is it held so late at night?"

"To make fun of the late meetings of the Clan, of course! Where have you come from? Across the great waters?" he laughed. He eyed the trio. "Where have you come from indeed...?" he added, though quietly and more to himself.

With great haste, Paul left the man. "Come now, Dawn, Arisbane. We must find a place to rest immediately. I fear I am not welcomed here," he whispered.

"Why? You are not a member of the Orion Clan, are you?" Princess Dawn asked.

Arisbane glanced at Paul and then at Princess Dawn. "Is it not obvious that he is? Only a member of the clan could have taken down a dragon with such ease as Paul!" she laughed.

"Why did you have to say that so loudly, Arisbane!?!" Paul hissed as all eyes turned upon him. "My friend! She is delusional! We were climbing the mountains when she lost her footing. She landed on her head! She does not know a single thing which she is speaking! Everyone is a member of the Orion Clan to her!" he told the crowd of eyes, hoping they would buy it.

"Look! He bears the mark upon his hand!" the same man whom he had just spoken to called out.

Paul tucked his hand behind his back once more. "I know not what mark you speak of!"

Before he could even say another word, however, a large group of men was upon him, beating him soundly. He tried to call upon the shadows for help, but every time he tried, someone else was holding him down, keeping him from moving.

Arisbane moved in to protect him, but she was far too weak and was pushed to the side with ease. She roared in frustration and anger. Princess Dawn stood by her side, too stunned to do anything but cry out over and over again, "My Paul, my Paul! Do not harm my Paul!"

"CEASE!" a voice rang out over the crowd.

Everyone stopped moving. One man continued to hold Paul perfectly still. Meanwhile, Paul continued to struggle against the weight of his attackers, though he was badly injured.

"What goes on here?" the man asked. It was obvious who he was for he adorned the finest furs and wore a golden crown encrusted with gems.

"This man is a member of the Orion Clan! The strange cat woman has told us so, and he bears their mark! He must be apprehended!" the same man told the King of the kingdom.

The King shook his head. "This is not how I wish for you to deal with such things. Bind him and send him off with my guard."

"Your Majesty! There is a misunderstanding! Paul would never belong to such a clan as the Orion's! He is a kind man, your Highness! He would never harm a living soul just for the sake of killing it!" Princess Dawn cried, trying to get closer to her dear friend.

"And why should I listen to what you have to say, peasant? Your word is but one against an entire village's! You would be wise to just give up your argument now, and I shall not place you under arrest as well!" he hissed, glaring at her.

"But, your Majesty! He is innocent!" she continued to argue.

The King rolled his eyes. "Well, since you do not seem to have any interest in my good will... Seize them both, guards!" he barked.

A knot of men advanced on Princess Dawn, surrounding her with ease and binding her arms behind her back. She opened her mouth to argue again, but one of the men shoved a wad of fabric into her mouth to keep her from speaking another word.

Paul attempted to kick at the guards as they began to bind his arms but continually missed. One guard hissed in frustration and anger before hitting him swiftly in the back of the head. After that, all went dark and the only thing Paul could feel was the weightlessness of being carried off.

CHAPTER 30

When Paul finally returned to his senses, he awoke to find Princess Dawn resting her head upon his chest and sobbing uncontrollably. "Oh, Paul! How could this happen to us? How, Paul? How? Arisbane was not taken, only us! Oh, why, Paul? Why? It just is not fair! I know you would never be one of those dastardly people whom the guards talked so rudely about! Say it is not so, Paul. Say it is not so!" she whispered hoarsely.

"I wish I could tell you it is not true, Princess Dawn, but I cannot tell a lie to you. You must understand that I love you with all my heart, but being a member of the Orion Clan was a birthright, and I was in no position to forsake it lest I be put to death!" Paul replied, rubbing his throbbing head. "I apologize, Princess Dawn. I never knew that it would hurt you so, but I am a member of the clan, and I cannot change that."

She shook her head. "No, Paul! You do not have to be a member of the clan! Forsake the clan, Paul! For our own sake! If you do not deny them, we shall certainly be put to death! Please oh please oh please, Paul! Do not trade me

144

for the Orion! It is not worth it, Paul! I shall stand by you no matter what, but the Orion will leave you! I know they will! Please! Just do it for me!"

"I can deny them verbally, but I could never actually leave the group. Not even for you."

"Then you do not love me, Paul! If you cannot give up one thing for me, how can I know that you truly love me? You do not, Paul! Why? Why would you pretend to love me all of those years but never actually go through with it?"

"I told you, Princess Dawn. I do lo-"

"No! You do not!" Tears choked out the rest of her words.

Paul reached up and wrapped his arms around her, but she shook them off violently. "If it pains you this much, I shall forsake them. You know that I love you more than anything in the world," he whispered.

"How am I to trust you, Orion slave?" she hissed.

"Then I shall seal my promise," he whispered, leaning over and giving her a kiss upon the lips.

At that, she finally allowed him to hug her. "Oh, Paul. You do not know how happy that makes me!" She was still crying, though it was no longer as profusely.

Within the moment, the door to the cell opened. "You are being called upon by the King. Your trial shall begin now."

Paul nodded curtly and helped Princess Dawn to her feet, brushing away her tears with his thumb. "Make sure that we argue that I never have nor will belong to the Orion Clan. I was born into the lineage, but I never agreed with nor did I accept the Orion Clan."

Princess Dawn's lip quivered, but still she nodded in agreement. "Very well, my knight," she whispered back.

The guard led Sir Paul and Princess Dawn to the throne room where a group of men were assembled. As the duo walked past them, they booed and scoffed at them, spitting at the ground by their feet. Paul clutched his fist and

145

prepared to strike one of the daring citizens, but the guard held him back and shoved him to the front of the room where he was forced to kneel before the King.

"Now... *Paul* as we have been told your name is. You have been brought before us because you have been accused of being a member of the accursed Orion Clan. What have you to say about this?" the King asked.

"I resent this accusation for I never have, nor will I ever, pledge allegiance to such a foul minded group as the Orion Clan. My loyalty lies solely with my King whom I gladly serve as a faithful knight under his coat of arms," Paul replied.

"And what say you, woman?" he asked, turning his attention to the woman kneeling before him.

"I can honestly vouch for him. He has always served his King and kingdom well, following the code of chivalry. I would know for I am the King's daughter," Princess Dawn stated.

"Of course you are. I am to believe that you, a ragged and filthy woman, are a Princess? Hardly any way for a Princess to keep herself..." the King said, chuckling. "Perhaps your King is merely the King of a vegetable patch!"

Her cheeks lit up with a blush of anger. "You dare question my lineage?"

The entire crowd joined in the King's laughter at that point. "Please, miss! Can you at least attempt to be serious in our court, unless you would like to put on the patch work clothes of our jester with the bells jingling with your every step? Then, be my guest! I shall not stop you!" he said.

Paul jumped to his feet. "The woman whom you berate is Princess Dawn of Asthla!" he hissed.

"Hardly! My son and I visited Asthla but a year ago to court the Princess Dawn! This woman looks nothing like her!" he said, glaring at Paul now.

"I speak the truth. I highly doubt that you would look very decent if you were kidnapped by a group of men and nearly fed to a dragon!"

There was a mere flicker of resentment in the King's eyes. "A group of men? Sounds like a fable."

"Your eyes tell me otherwise, your Majesty," he said, tapping into the thoughts of the King's shadow.

How could that boy have figured it out? Those Dawn Treaders must not have been as good as they claimed to be if they allowed a mere boy to discover that they were working for the King! This is ridiculous! Certainly they shall have to pay for this. They were supposed to bring Princess Dawn back here so that she might be forced to marry my son! the shadow thought.

"I might even be so daring as to say that you were the one who hired them to kidnap the Princess! You know this woman that stands before you is indeed Princess Dawn. You merely deny it to cover up your own tracks!" he said. He pulled out the note he had found in his room the day that Princess Dawn had first disappeared. "Your crest is even upon their ransom notes!"

The guard swiped the paper from the loud talking boy's hands and read it over. "He speaks the truth, your Majesty."

"So what? It is ever so possible that someone could steal my parchment," the King said, waving away the accusation.

"Is it also possible for your handwriting to be stolen as well?" the guard asked.

The King moved uncertainly in his seat. "It is possible that the Dawn Treaders could have copied my penmanship."

"I never told you the group's name was the Dawn Treaders," Paul pointed out.

The knot of guards held their weapons pointed at their King.

"Perhaps if you have lied to us about this, then you might have lied about other things as well." The head of the guards waved a hand at the duo who had been accused. "Leave now. You are proclaimed innocent."

"I am the King, and I say that these two are guilty!" the King hissed. "Treason!"

"Your word no longer matters. *You* are under arrest for treason against another kingdom whom we are not at war with!" the head of the guards replied.

"You cannot arrest your own King!"

"Just watch us!"

Paul and Princess Dawn slipped out before the altercation could grow even more heated. Arisbane was waiting for them outside. The noises of the fight could be heard through the stone walls.

"What is going on in there?" she asked.

"You do not wish to know. Now, come! We must leave this place at once!" he answered, grabbing her hand and pulling her away as they fled from the village.

CHAPTER 31

The small group did not cease running until they had reached the forest. Once there, they collapsed in a heap, lungs screaming for oxygen. They could already see the sun sinking below the horizon and shook their heads.

"How long were we held for? It felt like only a day, but my stomach begs to differ," Paul complained, clutching his aching gut. He felt as though he could eat an entire cattle of cows.

"No, no, Paul. You were there for three weeks, I'm afraid," Arisbane said, shaking her head slowly. "They wanted to hold the trial sooner, but whoever knocked you out hit you far too harshly. You were out cold for those three weeks."

"It cannot have been three weeks!" Paul gasped, shaking his head.

"Paul, it no longer matters!" Princess Dawn chimed in. "We are on our way home now, and that is what matters."

"But your father thinks that we are both dead!" he moaned, throwing himself down on the cold, hard forest ground.

149

"Why would he think that?" she quipped. "We have only been gone for a month!"

"I told the King that we would be back within a month's time. He shall think we are dead."

Princess Dawn's lower lip began to quiver. "No... No... He cannot possibly think that yet! We are still alive! There must be some way to get home and show him that we are still well and alive!" she cried. "He cannot think we are dead!"

"Unfortunately, we are still almost a week away from the kingdom. There is no possible way for us to make it back," he said as he wrapped his arms about her waist and held her closely. "Not even Umbra could carry us that quickly. Speaking of Umbra, though, where is he?" He turned his attention to Arisbane.

She clapped her hands and quickly whistled. Sure enough, Umbra came charging out of the forest and ran to his master's side. Playfully, he nudged the boy's head and snorted in his hair. His large eyes looked deeply into his own.

"I missed you, too, Umbra," he said, kissing the horse on its muzzle. He gently stroked the horse's head.

"What are we doing waiting around? Umbra is rested! He can carry us! We can still shave some time off!" Princess Dawn said, jumping to her feet.

"Can you do that for us, Umbra?" Paul asked.

The horse nodded its head and knelt down so that the two might climb atop him.

"Farewell, Arisbane!" he called over his shoulder to the cat woman.

She smiled and waved a clawed hand. "You get home in one piece, you hear me? I am not going to be around to protect you anymore. And consider yourself welcome in my forest any time!" she shouted after them.

Paul helped Princess Dawn up onto the horse's bare back before he kicked its sides sharply, and they took off as quickly as the horse could possibly move.

"We shall make it back to Father! I just know we will! And Father will be thrilled to have his daughter and best knight with him once more!" Princess Dawn said, kissing Sir Paul's cheek.

"Indeed he shall. And you will be glad to hear another bit of wonderful news," he replied, smiling broadly.

"What good news could you have for me?" she asked.

"Let us just say that the brook will not be the only one that knows we are in love anymore!"

"You mean... No! You cannot! That is not possible! Is it?"

"Upon our return, we shall become husband and wife," he said, answering her thoughts.

She tightened her arms around him and began to bounce, though not too much for they were still on the horse's back. "Oh, Sir Paul! Oh, *my* Sir Paul! I cannot believe it! How did you get him to agree?"

"He would have agreed to anything at the time. All he wanted was to have you home, safe and sound once more." He turned around slightly and kissed her gently on the cheek.

All she did was continue to hug him. "Oh, Paul... Sir Paul... Prince Paul... King Paul!" she mumbled as she tested out each name.

Paul merely laughed. Princess Dawn was so in love with him, and it made him feel terrible about lying to her that he would leave the Orion Clan when, in fact, he would not. There was no way he could put the two of them in danger like that by leaving the clan for the sole reason that she did not approve of it. After all, his allegiance was to the Orion Clan more than it was to her. True, he loved her, but his true passion was not in humans but in the hunt. He felt terrible for thinking as such, but it was true.

As he bantered this back and forth in his head, he grew completely unaware of what was truly going on. Within moments, he was fast asleep, his head resting upon his horse. Princess Dawn had also fallen asleep and was resting her head upon his back. Paul's rest was anything but restful, however.

CHAPTER 32

As Paul slept, visions of those who had passed away during his journey flashed before him. He could see the Dawn Treaders, the Guardian of the Mountain, even the King whom he presumed to be dead or at least close to it by that point. Even those who were still alive haunted his dream: that drunken man and the flirtatious inn keeper, the Guardian of the Mountain's child and the man whom had spoken to him at the fair. Had it not been for any of these people, he would not have been in the position he was in.

Nigel, Ethan, and Duane were predominant in all of his dreams. They constantly came back as a reminder of why he had been there and who he had become. His worst dream, however, was when he failed.

He was standing at the top of the mountain, alone with the Dawn Treaders. Nigel and Ethan were standing back while Duane came at him, a battle ax held high above his head. With all his might, Paul attempted to summon Duane's shadow to trip him once more, but it was all in vain. Nothing was happening. Every time he tried, the result was always the same: nothing! He looked up to the sky. Of course! The sun was blocked by a cloud! There were no shadows.

Duane was nearly upon him now. As he brought the ax down, Paul raised his daggers, catching it only a hair's breath away from his face. He shuddered as he backed up. Still, Duane came after him, battle ax held high above his head.

"Please, Duane! What are you doing? You know that you want nothing to do with me!" Paul cried out, knocking away the swings of the ax with his daggers.

"This is exactly what I want to do with you! You should be thanking me, after all. Your sweetheart has already moved on to the next world. Would you not like to join her in such a perfect world? A place where the two of you can be together for eternity?" Duane jested.

There was a pang in his chest. He was a demonic spirit. Princess Dawn was an angel on Earth. Surely, she went to Heaven, a place where he would never be welcome, not since he plotted with Lucifer. "Please! Say it is not so!"

"Ah, but it is! It is entirely so!" he laughed, swinging the ax once more.

Paul rolled out of its path, resting against a rock jutting out of the mountain floor. "No! Why? Why would you kill her?"

"I am only following Nigel's orders. Another order was to kill anyone who knew. That means you," he swung again, but this time he completely missed the mark.

Ethan rolled his eyes. "Get some decent aim, would you, Duane?"

"Shut up, Ethan. I do not see *you* doing anything over there!" he hissed.

"Take it easy big man!" he chuckled.

Nigel crossed his arms. "This is taking too long. Ethan. Give me your bow. I shall finish the boy myself." Before Ethan could even move, he snatched the bow and an arrow from him. "If you want something done right, ya got to do it yourself..." he mumbled to himself, letting the arrow fly. It was true to its mark, hitting Paul in the center of his chest.

"Forgive me, Princess Dawn..." he whispered. "Forgive me, Princess Dawn..."

"Forgive me... Forgive me, Princess Dawn..." he continued to groan. He awoke to a shaking on his shoulder.

"I forgive you, Sir Paul, though I know not why it is that I am forgiving you. Were you having a terrible dream? A horrid nightmare? My poor knight!" Princess Dawn whispered, pulling him into a hug. "I hope you are all right. Do not worry. All shall be well now. Remember: we are together again! Nothing can be wrong as long as I am with you and you are with me!" She pecked him with a reassuring kiss.

He blushed and smiled. "Thank you kindly, Princess."

"We are soon to be married. Please. Just call me Dawn," she said.

"Very well, Dawn," he said with a slightly bigger smile. He returned her kiss finally.

"I wish we could go even faster. We could have been wed by now, husband and wife, locked together in holy matrimony until the end of time!" she crooned.

"Alas, if our lives had not played out as such, we might never have been married. It was through misfortune that I was able to get your father to agree to our marriage. Now, speak no more of what is to come and what should have been. Rather, let us live in this moment. We are together now, and that is the only thing that we should focus on. Just the now and us," he explained.

She smiled and rested her head upon his shoulder. "Very well. If that is all that concerns you, then that shall be all that concerns me."

Umbra stopped finally and rested himself. Sir Paul and Princess Dawn used the time to eat and drink and simply be merry. Never had there been a happier couple than Paul and Dawn.

CHAPTER 33

So the duo rode on for the next few days, going and stopping as the horse chose to. It did not bother them that they were going slowly. Their love was kindling from the tiny spark that had been there when they were only eight to a now roaring forest fire that could consume anything in their path. They could conquer anything that came at them, as they had already proved.

When they finally reached Asthla, they were surprised to see how gloomy the town had become. It was no longer full of excited and chipper people, but, instead, it was full of dreary and dull peasants. Paul shook his head. "Apparently they do not know that their Princess is still alive."

A small girl walked over to them and grinned at them with a half toothy smile. "Dawn!" she chirped, pointing at the Princess upon the horse's back. "You Dawn!" She clapped her hands happily. "I met the Princess! The Princess!" She skipped around the horse gaily but tripped. Her lip began to quiver before she started bawling.

"Hush now, child," Princess Dawn whispered, jumping off the horse and hugging the girl.

She sniveled and looked up at her. "You nice, Princess Dawn. I like you! You nice ghost!" she giggled.

"I am not a ghost, child. I am very much alive," she assured her with a smile. She nudged the child's shoulder.

"You are not dead?" she asked, poking her arm.

"I am not dead."

She giggled and ran off. "Princess Dawn is here! Princess Dawn is here!" she shouted out to the world.

"Quite an adorable child. Perhaps we shall have one some day," Paul chuckled as he got off the horse. He took Princess Dawn by the hand and began to lead her to the castle.

Once there, the guards nearly fainted from the shock of seeing the two back alive. "Sir Paul! Certainly you are still with us!"

"Now why would I leave you knights when you know that you need me!" he laughed.

The two guards joined in on his laughter. "The King is in his throne room. Make haste to go see him. He shall be overjoyed to see his most wonderful child and his faithful knight home and safe."

Paul nodded. "Thank you, Sirs," he said, heading into the castle.

Inside, everything still looked as it had when he had left. However, Sir Asher was not at his usual post. It was a bit odd, but he figured he merely had business to take care of with the Orion Clan. Other than that, nothing struck him as out of the ordinary.

Before they entered the throne room, they could hear sobbing coming through the door. Princess Dawn chewed on her lip and glanced at Paul nervously. He gave her a reassuring nod, and they proceeded into the room.

"Your Majesty! I return bearing great news! I have found Princess Dawn, and she is alive!" Sir Paul called out to the grieving King.

The King looked up. His hand flew to his heart and his eyes that were already filled with tears were even more filled. "Princess Dawn! My child, my baby, my girl!" he cried, leaping from the throne and running over to greet her.

She ran out and met him half way, throwing her arms around his neck as though never to let go. "I have missed you so dearly, Father! I prayed daily that we might be reunited! Surely God was listening, for here we are!" she replied, kissing his cheeks.

"How could He not listen to you, my faithful child?" he asked, returning her kisses. "Oh, Dawn! I am certain Paul has told you the terms of your return. I hope you are not upset..."

"Father, I could not be happier! Sir Paul will make a most glorious husband and King when the time comes! I thank you a thousand times, Father! I love Sir Paul! I will marry him in a heartbeat!"

Sir Paul lowered his head. "I will be honored to marry your most lovely daughter."

"Come here, boy! Come closer," he said, holding out an arm to him.

He approached him slowly and was pulled into a hug with Princess Dawn. "I thank you kindly for accepting me into your family with such open arms," he said with a tiny laugh, glancing over at Princess Dawn.

"Oh, Father! When shall the wedding be?" Princess Dawn asked, grinning from ear to ear.

"Tomorrow shall be the day. I cannot make you two wait any longer." The King finally released the two. "Polish your armour, Sir Paul! You must be looking your finest when you are to be married!"

"Indeed. Until tomorrow, my Princess," he said as he bowed low and kissed the back of her hand.

"Arise, good knight. Until it be morrow!" She winked at him and moved her hand slightly in a watery movement.

He nodded. "I shall meet you then. Might I have a moment with your Father?"

Princess Dawn nodded and left. "What is on your mind, lad?" the King asked.

"Where is Sir Asher? Certainly he has returned," he replied.

"Alas, we have not seen him since your induction into the knighthood. He did not tell you where it was that he was going that he would be gone for so long, did he?" he replied.

Paul shook his head. "No. He did not. Ah well. I am certain that he shall return soon." He walked out of the room, joy filling his heart.

CHAPTER 34

As soon as the sun went down, Sir Paul left his chamber and headed out into the forest. Usually such a dark place at night, it seemed to be illuminated at the late hour. It was rather odd to him, but he did not care. He could see his Princess, and extremely soon to be wife, again. Thrilled as he was, he was still extremely nervous.

Princess Dawn was waiting for him by the brook once more, her smile even brighter than the sun had been. "Paul!" she chirped, running over to him and pulling him into a hug. "I cannot wait until tomorrow! How I wish we could be wed right now in front of the brook!"

"Then why not? We can do a fake wedding, just for the forest animals!" he said.

"What about for the Guardian of the Forest?" a voice asked from behind them.

"Arisbane!" the two cried out, turning around. "You are well!"

"Of course I am well! Did you not expect me to be fine?" Her tail twitched back and forth as her human face smiled at them. "So you two are to be married? I take it your father is all right?"

"All is well here now. The King was thrilled to see us. Our real wedding will not be until tomorrow," Paul explained.

"You should come! We would love to have you there!" Princess Dawn chimed in.

"I am afraid your kind is not all quite as accepting of me as you two have been or as the people by the mountain were. Their minds are not as open to the things which are not like they are. Do not take me wrong. I would love to attend. It is just for my safety as well as your own," Arisbane sighed.

He looked her over. "Can you not hide your ears and tail?" he asked. "After all, you have hidden almost all of your black fur. It should not be all that difficult."

"It is not that it is difficult, it is just that I do not like hiding who I am," she told him.

"Please, Arisbane? Can you do it for us? You have helped us so much! You should come to our wedding!" Princess Dawn pleaded.

With a sigh, she closed her eyes and her ears and tail shrunk away, human ears forming on the side of her head. "Do I look... human?" she asked.

They nodded eagerly. "Very much," Paul said. "So I take it you shall be joining us tomorrow at the castle?"

"Indeed, I shall," she said. Though for tonight, I must return to go get some more rest. See you both tomorrow, Mister and Missus Hunter!" she said, bowing to them before leaving.

"And now we are alone again," Princess Dawn said, laying down once more next to the brook. She pulled Sir Paul down with her.

"And that is how it should be with us and our brook," he whispered, kissing her gently upon the lips. He held her close and smiled.

They continued to spend the night in silence, listening as the brook recounted their epic tale while they rested. It spoke solely to them, only allowing them to comprehend its stories. Still, it referred to Paul as Victor and Princess Dawn as the Princess Dawnella. Unlike before in its original tale, it recounted the Dawn Treaders, or Dawn Slayers as it referred to them as.

After repeating the tale time after time again, it went on to speak of the wedding between "Victor" and "Princess Dawnella." It was not an epic as the other stories had been. Instead, this tale was certainly full of more love and joy. There was no apprehension, no upsetting events, only things that they wanted to hear about being together forever.

Princess Dawn pulled Paul even closer as they listened to the tale. When the brook reached the end of the tale, she whispered, "And they lived happily ever after. The end."

"It is not the end, but the beginning," he replied, kissing her gently.

She blushed and smiled. "That sounds like a far better way to end a story."

"Of course. Stories are never the end, but are always the beginning. There is never an end to anything, after all," he said.

"But what about death? Certainly there is not much to look forward to after you have left the Earth," she pointed out.

"Not even death is the end. It is a new beginning. Whether one should become an angel, a demon, or even a fallen angel, death will only lead them into a new beginning of life. Death never leads to the end," he continued to explain.

"Oh. I see. Well, certainly we shall become angels and live happily ever after together!" she chirped, pecking him on the neck with a kiss.

He remained silent at that point, for he knew that it would not be true. Never would God allow such a devilish

163

spirit to become an angel. However, his conscience knew that there was a great possibility that this, his human part, could join in the company of Heaven. Still, he was not entirely sure, for he had bargained with a spirit. He could only hope that he could go to Heaven to actually be with Princess Dawn himself rather than having to be with her through the demon spirit.

"We should probably return. It would not be well if one of us should fall asleep at the altar," he finally said.

"Indeed, that would be terrible. Come, my soon to be Prince and King," Princess Dawn replied, getting up from the ground and holding out her hand to Sir Paul.

He gladly took it and walked off with her. Once out of the forest, he gave her a final kiss. "Until tomorrow, my wife."

"Until tomorrow, my husband," she replied before running off toward her own room.

Meanwhile, Paul took his time in returning to his room. He highly doubted that he would be able to sleep with so much excitement going on the next day. Continually, he wrung his hands. He surely hoped that nothing would go wrong.

CHAPTER 35

Once the sun was above the horizon again, Paul arose from his bed and began to put on his suit of armour. Today was the day he had been waiting for! He was thrilled. Never had it crossed his mind that today would actually happen. The entire time he dressed, however, he waited to receive news from one of the other nobles saying that the Princess was nowhere to be found. Fortunately, such news never reached his ears, so he finished dressing and walked out of his room.

Many other nobles were rushing through the halls. Even Lord Ivan Averk was spotted running around making preparations, with a new page by his side that was sporting an all too familiar black eye. Mostly cooks and jesters were running around, trying to make sure that everything that they would need was in place. Out of the corner of his eyes, he saw a group of gypsy performers. He questioned why the King would hire such outcast people to perform, but he did not vocalize it. After all, the King knew best.

He found a break in the traffic and began to make his way to the throne room. Inside, a priest was already waiting, conversing with the King. Princess Dawn was nowhere in sight.

"Ah, young Paul! I see you have made it! You are a bit early, but no matter! I would like you to meet Brother Aaron," the King said as he motioned to the robed priest standing next to him.

"Good day, Brother Aaron," Paul said, nodding to Aaron.

"Greetings, lad. May God smile down upon this marriage," he replied, lowering his head slightly.

The group waited while the guests began to enter the room and stand off to the sides. Most of the guards were in attendance. A few stayed back so that they might guard the castle and the Princess. No one wanted to have a repeat of the kidnapping.

Finally, all guests had arrived, and Princess Dawn made her way down the center, clad in a lovely blue gown that brushed the floor as she walked. Within her hands she held a bouquet of brilliant orange flowers. She smiled at Sir Paul as she made her way to stand next to him.

"Dearly beloved! We gather here in the sight of God to join together Sir Paul Carson Hunter and Princess Dawn Ella Rayland in Holy Matrimony. Be there any here among you who feel as though the two should not be wed, speak now or forever hold your peace," Brother Aaron announced.

The crowd remained silent, so he continued with the ceremony. "Now I ask you who are to be married that if you should think of any reason that you should not be married upon this day, I ask you to speak out now, lest God put this marriage asunder."

Paul knew he had a reason, that he could not leave the Orion Clan to be with her, but he remained silent.

Upon the silence, he returned to the rites. "Sir Paul, will you take this woman to be your wife forever and always in this act of Holy Matrimony? To respect her, honour her, comfort her, and keep her, should she be in sickness or in health. And will you remain loyal to her as long as you both shall live?"

"I will," Paul answered.

"And Princess Dawn, will you take this man to be your husband forever and always in this act of Holy Matrimony? To respect him, honour him, comfort him, and keep him, should he be in sickness or in health. And will you remain loyal to him as long as you both shall live?"

"I will," Princess Dawn answered, looking deeply into Paul's eyes.

"Who is it that gives Princess Dawn to be betrothed?" the priest continued.

The King stepped forward with a smile and a tear in his eye as he placed Princess Dawn's hand in the priest's and stepped away. The priest passed her hand along to Paul whom grinned warmly at her.

"I, Sir Paul, take you, Princess Dawn, to be my wedded wife, to have and to hold. For better or worse, for richer or for poorer, I shall stand by you. Never shall I leave your side. Until death do us part. May this be God's will," Paul said.

"I, Princess Dawn, take you, Sir Paul, to be my wedded husband, to have and to hold. For better or worse, for richer or for poorer, I shall stand by you. Never shall I leave your side. Until death do us part. May this be God's will," Princess Dawn said.

The priest pulled out the rings for the two. "Dear Lord, bless these rings and those that shall henceforth wear them. May they be faithful and loving to one another. May they do thy will. Amen." He handed one of the rings to Sir Paul.

Paul placed the ring upon her thumb. "With this ring, I promise myself to you." He moved it to her index finger. "I shall honour you." Again, he moved it, this time to her ring finger. "And I give you everything I have." Finally, he put her ring upon her finger. "In the name of the Father, the Son, and the Holy Spirit. Amen."

The priest handed another ring to Princess Dawn.

Princess Dawn placed the ring upon his thumb. "With this ring, I promise myself to you." She moved it to his index finger. "I shall honour you." Again, she moved it, this time to his ring finger. "And I give you everything I have." Finally, she put his ring upon his finger. "In the name of the Father, the Son, and the Holy Spirit. Amen."

"Those whom God has joined together, let no man put asunder! I now pronounce you Prince Paul Carson and Princess Dawn Ella Hunter," the priest announced.

With exuberant joy, Paul pulled Dawn close and kissed her upon the lips. She returned the gesture and beamed up at him. "Now you truly are my Prince," she whispered.

"And soon I shall be your King," he replied before kissing her again.

The King stepped forward. "Welcome, my son," he said, clapping the boy on the shoulder. He turned to address the crowd. "Come! Let us feast, celebrate, and be merry on this most joyous of days!"

"Long live Prince Paul! Long live Princess Dawn!" the crowd exalted.

CHAPTER 36

The minstrel's music burst out throughout the crowd as the jester danced about in his patchwork outfit of rainbow colours, his bells ringing along to the merry ballads. Many in the crowd clapped along, cheering on the group. The gypsies attached miniature cymbals to their hands and helped keep a steady rhythm going. Many in the room were laughing and having a good time.

"See that boy? That new Prince? He was once my page," Lord Ivan Averk said, beaming proudly as he gained more and more attention as he spoke of the "valiant" things he and Paul and done when he had first joined into the knighthood.

Paul pulled Princess Dawn from her chair and moved out to the floor. "If you would not mind, jester," he said, placing a hand upon the young man's shoulder.

"Ah, the young Prince! He has touched my shoulder!" he swooned, mock fainting. He jumped up to his feet swiftly, bells jingling loudly. "The floor is yours!" he announced, skipping away.

Turning to the minstrel, he made a gesture and the song came to a close. A new song started, wordless and slow. He pulled Princess Dawn close and wrapped an arm around her waist and used the other to hold her hand. A few Lords and Ladies joined in on the slow dance, but many just stood and watched the bride and groom glide across the floors, looking like an angel and her shadow with their feet never once touching the floor.

"I love you more today than I did yesterday, but nowhere near as much as I shall love you come morrow," Paul whispered in his bride's ear.

"But you shall never love me as much as I love you, dear Paul," she replied, kissing him gently. She rested her head upon his shoulder as he continued to twirl with her around the floor of the banquet hall.

The song drew to a close, and the couples each bowed to their partners before walking off the floor and sitting down once more at the table.

The jester ran back in the room, bells ringing fiercely. With a single movement, he flipped through the air and landed upon the table in front of the bride and groom. "My consolations to the bride. Having to marry such a stick in the mud as Paul!" he said, bowing to the Princess.

The crowd began to laugh. Paul merely smirked, playing along with the jester. "And my condolences to the jester, whom shall have to put up with trying to entertain I, the stick in the mud!" he called back.

"Nonetheless, even the dead shall laugh!" he said, jumping from the table and sitting in Princess Dawn's lap. "Hi ya, sweet heart!" he crooned, kissing her.

"Jester..." Princess Dawn complained.

"What? No kiss for me? I am truly hurt..." he mumbled, getting up once more. "Yoo hoo! Kingy! How do you do? Come! Let us dance!" He pulled the King from his chair and began to twirl him around the floor while the minstrel played an upbeat song. Everyone laughed and clapped along to his routine.

The jester spun the King right back into his chair. "Phew! You are quite the dancer, King!" he said, wiping his brow. "I must retire for now! Do not miss me too much, Kingy!" He waved and did a few back flips until he was out of the room.

"I cannot believe you have to put up with him for so long... How can you possibly stand his terrible jokes and acts?" Paul asked Dawn.

"One grows used to his foolery. Besides, after a while, he tends to grow on you. He is not all that bad," she said with a shrug.

The King stood up at the head of the table, holding up his goblet of wine. "To the new Prince of Asthla! May he live long and well!" he cried out.

"To the Prince!" everyone cheered, lifting their own cups before downing the contents.

As the King sat back down, Paul arose from his seat. "I must thank you all for the kindness which you have extended unto me. This road has been long and difficult, but I thank the King for his support and I thank Princess Dawn for never giving up on me. Also, I must extend my gratitude to Arisbane. Without her, I fear I would have never found Princess Dawn."

Arisbane smiled from her spot not far down the table. She lifted her glass to Prince Paul.

"To Asthla!" he cried out.

"To Asthla!" everyone else cheered, clapping their hands and whooping loudly.

The minstrel began to play once more while the guests began to feast. Like small children, Paul and Dawn clasped hands secretly beneath the table as they ate.

"Oh, Princess Dawn. This is the most perfect day I could have ever asked for," he whispered.

"Even with all of these people around? Tell me, Prince Paul, where are your parents? Certainly the King would have asked them to come," she said, looking up at him.

"Sadly, my parents have both passed on. The King was well aware. For if they were alive, I am certain that he would have postponed the wedding until a later date when my parents could have attended," he replied, shrugging his shoulders. "It has been a long time since I have gotten to see either of them..." he sighed.

She pulled him into a gentle hug. "Poor dear," she mumbled, kissing his cheek. "Dwell not on your sorrowful past! Let us look forward to the bright future! After all, the sun will not rise if it never set at all."

Paul raised an eyebrow. The line from his mother's lullaby?

"You sang it to me, back by the brook so long ago," she said, whispering the rest of the lyrics to him.

He smiled and held her even closer, though making sure that neither would fall from their chairs and embarrass themselves. When Princess Dawn finished the song, she glanced back up at him. "Shall we visit our dear friend the brook tonight?" she asked.

Slowly, he shook his head. "It is our first night as husband and wife. I would love to spend it here in the castle. The brook can wait until tomorrow to hear our news, can it not?"

She laughed. "Very well. Then come tomorrow we shall visit it once more. For now, let us dance some more! I have little appetite for this food!" she said, pulling him once more from his seat.

The crowd watched on as the duo danced. The gypsies gathered around and joined in, clashing their tiny cymbals and beating on stretches of deerskin. They moved in circles around the married couple, singing along with the minstrel in merriment.

The two laughed and held each other close as the music continued on. And so it proceeded until well into the night when the crowd departed. Last to leave was Arisbane.

"Good bye, my friends. Hopefully I shall see you both again soon," she chirped. She gave them each a quick hug before running off.

CHAPTER 37

Scarcely a year had gone by since the wedding when the King had come down with a severe illness. He was lying in bed, barely holding onto his life, when his daughter walked in with Paul. The two looked at him and exchanged a single glance. They knew that his time was drawing to an end. Even God was crying on that night, for the rain was falling down from Heaven in large droplets to the ground.

Princess Dawn walked up to him and clutched his cold hand in her own. "Please, Father. Say this is not the end! Fight against this disease! Do not leave us yet, Father!" she moaned, trying to keep tears from escaping her eyes.

Prince Paul stood on his other side, kneeling down beside him. "You have always been such a strong man. Certainly you can make it through this," he whispered.

The King took a deep, raspy breath. "Alas, I fear that this is one thing that I cannot defeat. I am terribly sorry, my daughter and my son, but I will not be able to be in this world much longer. God is calling me home to Heaven. I can nearly see it now."

That was far too much for Princess Dawn, and she collapsed upon his chest. "Oh, Father! No! You cannot say such things! Banish such thoughts from your mind! You shall live and all shall be well! You are not dying! Please! Get better, Father! Conquer this ailment!" she cried out, sobs racking her entire body.

"I cannot, my dear, dear daughter. My time has come to a close. I am sorry..." He slowly turned his head toward Paul. "You two shall be my successors. Do not let the kingdom dwell upon this terrible day. Instead, help them to look forward to the bright future they shall have with a young new King and a bright Queen. Promise me you shall work hard at preserving the kingdom! Please. That is my dying wish."

"I promise that I shall keep your kingdom with Princess Dawn," he whispered.

A small smile spread across his lips. "You are a good boy, Paul. You really are. Oh, how I wish I could have gotten to be with you more, to get to know you even better. Alas, it seems I shall not. I can see God's face now. He is calling to me. Farewell, Paul." He turned back to Princess Dawn. "Stay strong, my dear." With those words, his eyes closed and all was still.

She blinked repetitively. "Father?" she asked. When no response came, she began to shout. "Father!?! Father!?!" Her fists pounded against his motionless and lifeless chest. "No, Father! I will not let you die! Open your eyes, Father! Breathe the air! Do not just lay there!" Tears streamed down her cheeks.

Swiftly, Paul crossed to the other side of the bed and pulled her into a hug. "I am afraid he will not be coming back, my Princess," he whispered, gently rubbing her back. "We shall take over for him. All shall be well. Do not worry about a thing."

"How can I not worry? Not only have I lost my mother years ago, but now I have lost my father as well! Oh,

Paul! I know not how to cope with such losses. They are not like anything I have gone through before." She continued to cry into his shoulders. Her shoulders shook violently.

"You will learn to cope one day, dear Dawn. Perhaps it shall not be today, but one day you will overcome this grief. Remember what I told you, Dawn. Death is not the end, it is merely a new beginning. Always remember that. Someday, you shall be reunited with your father, but, for now, you two must spend some time apart, and you shall be with me." He gently kissed her upon the lips. "Now come, Dawn. We must go find the elders and address them about what has occurred so that we might make arrangements for a coronation ceremony as well as a funeral."

With a shaking sigh, Princess Dawn nodded and rose from the floor, Paul with her. They walked out of the room and took only one final quick glance at the King's body. Its disposal was the least of their worries.

After a few moments of searching, they found the elders in their chambers, discussing the King's well being. The two exchanged worried looks before approaching the group.

"I am afraid we bear terrible tidings for you, most honoured elders," Paul declared, lowering his head.

The elders looked over. "Come now," the oldest said. "What news have you to bring that it cannot wait?"

"We have just been in the King's chamber, and he has passed on to the next life," he said, keeping his head lowered.

There was a collective gasp among the elders as they began to sputter out questions. Again, it was the oldest one to calm them and speak to Paul in a cool and collected voice. "We extend our condolences to the two of you in the loss of your father," he replied. "There is not much time that we can spend tarrying on this. All of this useless banter will get us nowhere. In a week, we shall host your coronation, but not before then. The news must first be spread and the King given a proper burial."

Princess Dawn choked back tears. Slowly, Prince Paul patted her on the back. "We shall do all that we can to aid you in this," he stated. "Whatever you wish for us to do, we shall."

"For now, there is nothing you can do save give us time. Take charge of the King's duties, and come next week, we shall crown you," he said, bowing his head to the Prince.

"Thank you, dear elders." He wrapped his arm around Princess Dawn's shoulders and led her from the room. "Come, my Queen. Let us make preparations for next week."

She nodded slowly and allowed him to take her out of the room.

CHAPTER 38

The coronation went on without a single flaw. This was great news for the new King and Queen, for far too much had been going wrong in their lives. Only one other bit of news brought joy to the couple, and that was that the Princess was with child. This was the greatest news of all, and it made the coronation ceremony much more joyous than it would have been otherwise.

There was no feast held afterward. The couple was not in the mood to host a party. Even the jester knew better than to approach the two and try to put a smile upon their faces. He simply watched them with a sad look upon his face. There was no joy in a jester if their masters were not looking for it, and Paul and Dawn were certainly not looking for any of his jokes and joy.

That night, as Queen Dawn lay in her bed, she looked over at Paul. "Tell me, my King. Why will you not come and lie down with me tonight?" she asked as he began to head out the door.

"I have business to take care of, my Queen. I shall return before morning," he said, brushing off her question.

She sighed. "Do not be gone long!" she begged.
"I promise I will be back shortly." With that, he walked out and into the forest.

By the time he walked into the forest and down the secret tree, the Orion Clan meeting had already begun.

"Paul!" Mistress Ehiztaria scolded. "You cannot continually show up late to our meetings! Ever since you got married, you tend to forget."

"I am sorry, Mistress Ehiztaria. Today was the coronation ceremony, and it ran a little late. I had to put Queen Dawn to rest before I could leave," Paul said, lowering his head.

"Remember, *King* Paul. Your loyalty lies first in the Orion Clan, then in the affairs of your heart. Not vice versa. When was the last time you even went on a hunting expedition into the forest?" she asked, glaring at him coldly.

"Indeed it has been a long time since I have been able to go out on a hunt, but I promise that I shall be more loyal. Please, accept my apologies." He kept his head down.

She hissed. "You have until the next meeting to straighten up. Your uncle was so much different from you! Oh, the loyalty *he* had toward us! He took his loyalty straight to the grave!"

Paul's head shot up. "Asher has died?" he asked with a gasp.

"I sent him out on a simple expedition. He never returned, so he shall be henceforth assumed to be dead," she said, waving off the question.

He shook his head. So that was what had happened to his uncle! Or, at least, that's what they *said* happened to his uncle. "I do not feel well. Perhaps I should not stay..."

"Sit down, Paul. Do not leave this room until the meeting has come to a close. Do you understand me, young man? Stay here!" Her eyes were lit with anger.

With a moan, Paul sat down in an empty chair, shooting daggers at Mistress Ehiztaria with his eyes.

179

She rolled her eyes and went on with the meeting. "So, as you are all well aware, we will be going on another expedition after this meeting and we shall search for some creatures that have been spotted by the brook. Among them are a winged horse and a basilisk. Certainly they shall be easy prey. Especially for those of us who have been dedicated." The last sentence was directed solely at Paul.

He rolled his eyes in disgust and waited for the meeting to adjourn.

At the end, Mistress Ehiztaria approached him once more. "Come with my hunting group and serve your clan, Paul," she told him before leaving.

Paul arose from his chair and followed the knot of men and Mistress Ehiztaria out of the room and up the stairs of the tree hideout. "You will obey my orders, or else you shall all be dead. Is that understood?" Paul hissed at the group.

"Like we should listen to you!" Mistress Ehiztaria scoffed. "You will obey me! It does not go the other way."

"Oh, indeed?" he asked, raising his hand and closing it in a fist. The shadows rose from the ground and wrapped themselves around her.

"You really shouldn't be doing this, Paul," Mistress Ehiztaria warned. She managed to shoot a single arrow at him. It merely scraped his shoulder.

"Foolish old woman. You did not think I would take orders from you forever, did you? I've never really been one to have a power over me," he laughed. He allowed the shadows to tighten until the life left Mistress Ehiztaria's eyes.

"Stand down, Paul! We do not want to hurt you!" one man of the clan said, holding his sword pointed at Paul's throat.

"Do you wish to end up as Mistress Ehiztaria? I think not. Now, you shall all obey me or else I certainly will kill you all," he hissed.

"Why should we listen to one of the things we would kill in an instant?" he retorted.

"Because who better knows the way of magic than one who can use it?"

The men bowed to him. "All hail Master Paul!" they chanted.

"That is more like it. Now, come. We have a hunt to complete." He completely ignored the dead body of the former leader of the Orion Clan and led the group out to the brook. What he found there, however, he could never have been prepared for.

CHAPTER 39

Queen Dawn had left the castle and now lay by the brook, her hand resting tenderly upon her extended stomach. "Oh, Paul..." she whispered. "Why do you keep running away? Why can you not just stay for one day? Maybe even two? Three? Why would you leave me here to struggle on alone?"

Completely unawares to her, Paul was kneeling in the bushes nearby with his men. "Stay quiet!" he ordered.

A large cat stalked out into the clearing and transformed into an almost human form. "What ails you, my Queen?" she asked.

"Alas, Arisbane. It is Paul. He has left me once more. Still he refuses to tell me where it is that he runs off to," she sighed.

Arisbane sat down beside her. "You must not dwell upon these things of sorrow. I am sure that he shall return to you. Perhaps he is preparing some sort of surprise?"

"Unlikely. He is not one for surprises. If only he were. Then I would not worry about his so much! Oh, Arisbane! What am I to do?"

"Do nothing. Only wait for him," she replied. Her ears twitched. "Someone is near."

"Greetings, Queen Dawn!" Paul called out, leaving the bushes. He motioned to the others to stay put, despite how badly they wished to run out and slay the cat woman. "What brings you here?"

"I might ask you the same thing," she hissed.

"I came out here to be alone. That is all. For you," he said, plucking up some flowers from behind him without her noticing. He passed them over to her.

A tiny smile played across her lips. "Perhaps you are not all bad."

"I am not bad at all. I assure you of that!" He sat down beside her and gently kissed her stomach. "I cannot wait to meet our child."

"You must be patient with such things," she whispered. There was a quiet sound above them and she gasped. "Look, Paul! Pegasus!" she cried out, watching a winged horse fly over head.

No amount of orders could keep the Orion Clan hidden now. They burst forth from the bushes, some aiming up at the sky while others aimed for the cat woman.

Queen Dawn shrieked and hid behind Paul. "What are these men doing here!?!" she cried out. "Why oh why is the Orion Clan here!?!"

"I am sorry," Paul mumbled, hanging his head in shame.

She punched him. "How dare you! You told me you would leave! You told me that you would be true! You liar!" she hissed, running from the brook.

"Wait! Dawn! I...!" he gasped. He turned to glare at the men. "Was that worth it?" he hissed.

"Paul!" Arisbane cried out.

Quickly, he turned on his heels, but it was too late. One man had shot her with an arrow through the stomach and she was beginning to cough up blood.

183

"Thanks a lot, Paul," she cried out. "I thought I could trust you as well! Apparently, no one can! I hope you die! You hear me, Paul!?! DIE!!!" With that final utterance, her breathing came to a halt.

"You idiots!" he scolded the men. They ignored him as they retrieved the fallen cat woman and winged horse. "You blundering fools! I did not order an attack! See what you have done?" The shadows around him began to quiver with his increase in anger. "Why did you kill her?!?"

None of the men answered. The only thing they did do was flee for fear of their own lives.

Paul screamed at the top of his lungs, causing every creature within the wood to stir and run as far away as possible. Certainly he would need to teach all of those members of the clan a lesson, but that needed to wait until a later time. Now, his only concern was getting home to his wife to try and salvage their marriage, or at least what was left of it.

The clouds blew over the forest and Asthla once more, dropping torrential amounts of rain. He growled like a canine and pulled up the hood of his cloak to keep himself dry. With hunched shoulders, he stalked out of the forest, keeping his eyes solely on the path ahead. All he wanted was to be back with Princess Dawn. He wanted to make everything well. Unfortunately, that moment was never to come. There would be no way to ever patch this terrible deed up.

CHAPTER 40

"My Queen?" Paul whispered as he walked into their bed chambers. There was no response, nor could he find any sign that Queen Dawn had been there. With a sigh, he moved on to his old bed chambers. Nothing in that room had been touched either.

Frustration began to rise in him as he continued to look in room after room for a sign of his love, his wife, his life, but he could find no sign in any of these rooms. After visiting many rooms including the throne room, dining hall, and kitchen, he finally ventured into one final room: her father's bed chambers. The blankets were rather bulging. He ran over.

"Oh, my Queen! I have found you! Please! Wake up! Allow me to apologize for I am terribly sorry!" he cried out.

The covers did not move in any form of response.

"Do not do this to me, Dawn! Please! Arise! For Victor! Please, my Dawnella! Do not let this be the end! Dawn!" He quickly threw back the sheets to find nothing but a mere note, folded up with greatest care.

The words within made him gasp and drop the paper, for it read:

Not so Dear Paul,
I hope you are happy with you decision to be with the Orion Clan rather than myself. It was for your love alone that I remained here, but because you do not wish to love me in return, I no longer have a reason to stay. I hope that your lies were worth it and that you enjoy life without me, because now you will never receive a second chance. Hopefully, I will never see you again in life or in death. Some day, I shall go to Heaven and your spirit shall be forced to walk the Earth for the rest of eternity! May this letter serve as our divorce and my final testament.
With the love you never showed me, Dawn Ella Rayland, ex Hunter and our child-to-be

Paul shook his head slowly. "No..." he whispered over and over again. "Why, Dawn? Why? I could have made it up to you!" A sudden wave of rage engulfed him and he snatched up the paper. It was on the floor in a million tiny shreds within moments. "Have it your way, Dawn! Enjoy your new life while I alone shall rule on!"

Swiftly, he stormed down the stairs to the dungeons where his father remained chained. He balled up a fist and sent it flying right into the defenseless man's chest. "Idiot!" he hissed.

Sir Laurence merely shook his head. "What is it that I have done to you, Paul? I have merely been down here. I could not possibly have done you any harm!" he sighed.

"I should have learned from you that love meant absolutely nothing! What a fool I was! I cannot believe that I even believed that I could ever find true love!" he continued to yell, taking out his frustration on his father.

"Please, Paul. Can we not just talk it out?" he begged, trying to dodge the blows, but to no avail. "Why, Paul? Why?"

"I have learned my lesson now about love! There is no such thing! Love is a waste of time! It gets one nowhere! Just look where it got you!"

"You have it all wrong, son. Love is not a waste!"

"If it is not a waste, than why did Dawn leave? I loved her, and she loved me, yet she fled!"

"I am sure there is more to this than you are stating."

"There is not! She is gone! Curse you, Father! Curse you!"

Sir Laurence gave up on the argument. There was no use in it. Paul was stuck in his way, even if his way was illogical and made little sense at all.

Paul stormed back up the stairs, slamming the door behind him. Fierce thunder began to rumble throughout the sky as lightning pierced the clouds. The boy ran outside and stood in the midst of it all, glaring up at the sky. "What is the matter? Have I not been tormented enough? Perhaps she could have finally saved my soul!" he shouted up at the sky.

"Alas, be that as it may, I shall reign victorious, alone! The world shall be mine and mine alone!" he continued to cry out. "Starting with this pathetic city!"

Despite all of these claims, when he awoke the next day, he returned to being kind on the outside. There was no sense in causing an uprising. He needed trust to take over the world. By giving this place a false sense of security, he would easily be able to crush them.

He went to the elders and told them that the Queen had mysteriously disappeared. It was true, for he knew not where she had gone off to, but he wished he did know.

Still, he reigned over both Asthla and the Orion Clan, keeping them under an iron grasp. Never would he let one stray. Though he wanted world domination, his priority was to find his sister, Ammira. She would need to die. After all, she was the first to remove someone near and dear to him from his life.

He knew there would never be a happy ending for him, only one full of misery. But that did not bother him in the least. After all, he had already been a tormented soul for centuries. What did it matter that he would have to spend even more time as such?

As he watched the sun go down on yet another day, he whispered, "I shall find you, Ammira Laura Hunter, but you had better pray that I never do. It's the only thing that will save you."